Here's What the Critics Said:

"An ingenious spy story, with an ending which is both extraordinary and utterly right."

Atlantic Monthly

"Penetrating and ironic, a moving and convincing story . . . Boulle is a master of paradox."

New York *Herald Tribune*

"Taut with cool suspense, not a word is wasted."

St. Louis *Post-Dispatch*

"Cunningly contrived, rapid in pace, and shrewd in dialogue. Start the book . . . you'll finish it!"

Chicago *Sunday Tribune*

"An unusual and thoughtful book."

Saturday Review

"A first-class thriller . . . the tension, both moral and material, is magnificently sustained throughout."

London Times Literary Supplement

NOT THE GLORY

By the author of The Bridge Over the River Kwai
and Planet of the Apes

PIERRE BOULLE

MANOR
BOOKS
INC.

A MANOR BOOK 1974

Manor Books Inc.
329 Fifth Avenue
New York, New York 10016

 Published by
arrangement with Vanguard Press.
Printed in the U.S.A.

Library of Congress Catalog Card Number: 55-10687

"The deed is everything, not the glory."

JOHANN WOLFGANG VON GOETHE

NOT THE GLORY

PART ONE

1 The war had not put an end to the weekly dinner parties Sir Wallace and Lady Goodfellow gave for a small group of old and valued friends. It had simply endowed these evenings with a certain degree of austerity, which the elderly baronet's young wife regularly dismissed with an engaging murmur of apology: "There's war on, you know." She would follow this remark with a sigh and a smile. Her sigh conveyed the true value of the small piece of cheese that was to be seen on each guest's plate; her smile made them forgive the watery Irish stew, the lack of butter, and the somewhat specialized turn of the conversation.

There was a war on. Ever since this state of exception had been declared between the Anglo-Saxon world and the Teuton, Lady Goodfellow had conscientiously proscribed diamonds or emeralds in her drawing room. Silk stockings were only just allowed, but these had become more and more of a rarity and were regarded as a sign of bad taste. The ladies had yielded to the demands of the day. Jewels lay hidden away in safes. Evening dresses had been superseded by dark tailored suits that did not look too out of place beside the uniforms of the women's services. In this way a sense of unity was maintained even in outward appearances. It was really a rather rewarding sight.

Dinner jackets had been carefully put in moth balls and stored away for the duration. The gentlemen did not complain but cheerfully waited for the day when they could decently resume an outward appearance of respectability. They now wore dark suits, preferably as shabby as possible. A good piece of mending was a mark of good citizenship, and one Cabinet minister even prided himself on the number of darns in his socks.

"There's a war on, you know. . . ." Sir Wallace, Member of Parliament and Chairman of the National Recovery League, used to go to the office in a baggy brown suit adorned with patches. This suit was now the subject of legend. Some of his colleagues said he had borrowed it from a House of Commons porter, but that he changed into something else as soon as he got home, since his wife would not let him appear in it in private. Harmless jokes of this kind were good for morale. For a dinner party, however, Sir Wallace dressed fairly decently—there were limits, after all! His guests, too, had sufficient tact to maintain a certain standard of decorum. Their linen gleamed in all its pristine purity. Their collars were spotless and starched to perfection. National unity did not preclude individual self-respect. Lady Goodfellow's charm was in no way decreased by the simplicity of her clothes.

High spirits were not considered out of place at these parties, provided they were indulged in according to the rules. Sometimes even excesses were not frowned on. One night, during a raid in which an entire district of London was destroyed, Lady Goodfellow, the lovely, enchanting Lady Goodfellow (who was also, however, the serious-minded and strong-willed wife of the head of the National Recovery League, the symbol of composure and restraint) had proved her fortitude and initiative by launching one of these saturnalia herself. While the guests were trying to show some interest in a technical discussion of the merits of reinforced-concrete air-raid shelters, which Sir Wallace was expounding, their young hostess had suddenly stood up—some reports stated she had even thumped the table with her fist, uttering something that sounded almost like an oath—and had gaily declared that a few bombs were no excuse for graveyard manners, that Hitler would be only too pleased if he knew that his engines of war had disturbed London's normal equanimity, that to pull a long face at a time like this was tantamount to showing a disgraceful lack of faith in the destiny of the Empire and the sagacity of the Sovereign, that there were still four bottles of Burgundy stored away in the sideboard, that she would never be able to forgive herself if a bomb came down and smashed this precious hoard, and that here at last was a perfect opportunity to safeguard them for good by drinking them all at once in a toast to victory.

A foreigner would have condemned such behavior. In the first place, he would have disapproved of the spirit behind it, of the idea of celebrating such a mournful occasion by a binge. No doubt he would also have been rather astonished at such an ingenuous display of ignorance concerning the proper treatment of Burgundy. But Lady Goodfellow's guests, being British, were not in the least shocked by the motive behind the proposal or by the proposal itself. At one o'clock in the morning, after a lot of sour lemonade, each of the guests consumed his share of vintage Pommard. Their morale was thus raised, and they danced and sang till dawn. A number of toasts were proposed and some jovial comments made about the Chancellor of the Third Reich and his Air Marshal. In the morning the empty bottles were carefully collected for the benefit of National Recovery. In many British households the worst raids had been faced in this manner.

One evening in December, 1941, however, the little group of friends looked dejected. There was no trace of humor, and any sign of cheerfulness would have been considered in bad taste. Despondency clutched at their hearts. One old gentleman, a die-hard Tory, happened to be wearing a colored handkerchief in the breast pocket of his suit, which was otherwise, however, suitably shabby; Lady Goodfellow gave him such a withering look that the poor fellow went quite red in the face, muttered a few words of apology, and hastily pushed this unseasonable piece of finery out of sight.

Bad news had lowered everyone's spirits. A national disaster had put England into mourning: The finest battleship in the world, the *Prince of Wales,* pride of the Royal Navy, had just been torpedoed and sunk off Singapore by Japanese aircraft. *H.M.S. Repulse* had gone down in the same engagement.

The British had faced defeat in France without faltering. They had derived new strength from the threat of invasion. They had cracked jokes while the bombs fell. The most severe restrictions had not combined to disrupt their steadfast outlook. The reverses they had undergone in the Western Desert had done nothing more than kindle a feeling of admiration for General Rommel. The losses they had suffered in convoy scarcely affected them at all—that was all in the rules of the game. America's entry into the war they had clearly regarded as a counterbalance to the situation in the Far East: the Japanese invasion of Malaya, the advance on Singapore, and the critical position of that so-called impregnable bastion—all these were part of the countless battles that had to be lost before final victory could be won. Churchill had repeatedly said so, and the British public patiently agreed with him. But the loss of the *Prince of Wales* could not be so easily dismissed. It was like a manifestation of divine wrath, which deprived them of all spiritual sustenance and abandoned them to despair.

In this suicidal atmosphere Sir Wallace gloomily asked whether anyone could explain how it had happened. A young naval officer, whose uniform alone entitled him to a place in this exclusive gathering, gave them a short account according to the latest reports. He did his best to mitigate the blow by explaining that the famous battleship had not been sunk in a naval engagement but in an attack by aerial torpedoes. He told them how the Flag Officer, Admiral Sir Tom Phillips, had proved himself worthy of the finest traditions; how, knowing the end to be in sight, he had asked for his uniform cap to replace his tin helmet and, after giving the order to abandon ship, had himself gone down with his charge into the China Sea; how the survivors—"fine fellows, every one of them"—threshing about in a layer of oil that in some places was eight inches thick, and almost choking in the heavier fuel oil, had paid a last tribute to the "Old Lady" and their Admiral by singing "God Save the King," until both she and he had disappeared beneath the waves; how they had shaken their fists at the Japanese airmen who machine-gunned them in the water, using swear words of which even the first letter could not be uttered in the presence of ladies; how they had finally welcomed their own fighter planes, which did not appear over the scene of the disaster until twenty minutes after the action had taken place, with a volley of equally unrepeatable oaths. For the fact of the matter was that the disaster was due to absence of air protection. The honor of the Royal Navy was therefore unimpaired.

These details might have successfully restored the gathering's confidence if it had been a question of a less significant ship. But the *Prince of Wales* was a significant ship. She was the pride of the realm; and in addition to the glory of being one of the most powerful ships in the world, she was splendidly associated with an event of historical importance: on board this mighty battleship the fate of two great nations had been decided—when Churchill and Roosevelt held their first meeting. Her majestic arrival at Singapore a week before had been acclaimed throughout the Empire as a symbol of the firm determination to put those nasty little yellow men in their place.

The atmosphere of gloom and despondency persisted. Colonel Field, of the War Office, even went so far as to criticize Sir Tom Phillips' conduct on this particular occasion, putting forward an argument that almost convinced some of the other guests.

"My point is this," he explained. "It costs the State a

great deal of money for a man like Sir Tom Phillips to reach his present rank and acquire his experience. He's therefore worth a capital sum that he has no right to throw away, especially in time of war."

It was an argument that carried some weight, and the gentlemen without exception subscribed to the Colonel's opinion. "There's something in what he says, you know. . . ." But the ladies disagreed. With a fervor that brought the blood to her cheeks, Lady Goodfellow declared that the Admiral had chosen the only course of conduct that was decently possible in view of the magnitude of the disaster and the traditions of the Royal Navy. Colonel Field stuck to his guns and made a quick mental calculation to determine how much in hard cash Sir Tom had been worth at this stage in his career. The young naval officer protested, with all due respect, against this manner of assessing a man's value and called to mind a number of glorious instances in the past. Lady Goodfellow gallantly supported him. But Sir Wallace was impressed by the logic of the Colonel's argument. Besides, as head of the National Recovery League, he could hardly be expected to approve of any form of waste, even that of an admiral. He therefore declared rather sharply that this was a serious business and women knew nothing about it. The lady of the house emphatically denied this claim. Anxious for the support of a really reliable authority to put an end to this heated argument, Sir Wallace then invited William Conrad to give his opinion. Looking hard at the young naval officer, but not daring to look at his wife, Sir Wallace said, "We should like to have the verdict of someone really reliable, who knows how to deal with the realities of the moment and who, being born and brought up abroad, has been spared the effects of an education that in many respects is absurdly romantic."

It was an embarrassing situation, but William Conrad handled it with his usual subtlety and tact. Being of Polish origin, he explained, his views on naval tradition were necessarily rather limited. "All the same," he went on, "the death of a man like Sir Thomas Phillips can't simply be written off as an ordinary loss. You have calculated his value in hard cash. To be fair, you ought also to make a similar assessment of the increase in effort that his conduct will encourage in every branch of the service and of the spirit of revenge that his example is bound to instill. Both these factors ought to be taken into account."

Since the gentlemen, even Colonel Field, readily agreed that "there was something in what he said," a ray of comfort was provided by the guest of honor's well-chosen reply. Lady Goodfellow flashed a smile of gratitude in his direction, and William Conrad basked in its sunshine.

As soon as dinner was over, Conrad went up to his hosts, uttered a few words of thanks, and quickly left. Lady Goodfellow explained his abrupt departure: "These journalists have to keep the most impossible hours. There's an article of his coming out tomorrow that has to be finished tonight. Something rather important."

Colonel Field then redeemed himself in the eyes of the ladies by declaring that no one could have any doubt about the importance of William Conrad's articles and that men of his caliber were few and far between. In incisive terms, which a foreigner would quite wrongly have attributed to the presence of some opposition, he added that the conduct of this Pole since the beginning of the war should be held up as an example to every British subject, and that his talent as a writer was equaled only by his gallantry on the field of battle.

These words met with a murmur of approval. Sir Wallace went ever further and said that qualities like Conrad's were just what was needed in the present rather tricky situation, and that it was lamentable that such a first-class man should be prevented by his foreign birth from occupying a high-level official position. This view summed up the general feeling; and as soon as it was expressed, the ladies and gentlemen felt a little more cheerful at finding a topic of conversation on which they could all agree. They therefore exploited it to the full as they each drank a few drops of the sugarless coffee that the lady of the house passed around.

2

The Goodfellows lived in a small house in South Kensington. In spite of his bad leg, Conrad decided to walk all the way to his newspaper office off the Strand. He could get there by eleven o'clock, which would give him plenty of time. The excuse he had made to leave the party was really a white lie. His article was already finished; he had only to read it over and correct it, which would take him no more than an hour. The truth was that he had suddenly felt an unaccountable urge to be alone. He was in no hurry. He loved prowling about the streets of London at night, when the grime of the old city was no longer an affront. He inhaled the icy fog almost with enjoyment and set off as briskly as was possible in the black-out.

The memory of the conversation that evening brought a slightly reproachful smile to his lips. He asked himself whether he was really deriving any benefit from these people. He had to admit, however, that no fault could be found with their environment so long as Sir Wallace's charming wife graced it with her presence. As often happened when he was alone and had nothing else to do, he went over in his mind the course he had traced since his arrival in London and recalled, with a certain amount of self-satisfaction, some of the events in his brilliant career, events that Lady Goodfellow was forever describing to her little group of friends and which that very night she was recounting yet again to an audience in no way put out by a story they had already heard a hundred times before.

William Conrad had not had the good fortune to be born a British subject—a fact that had already been deplored that evening. Although his English was perfect and he wrote it like a genius, a foreign intonation in his speech all too often betrayed his misfortune. He had been born in Danzig. His mother came from Scotland, it was true, but his father was Polish. He had turned up in London in 1935 after two years of persecution at the hands of the new Nazi leaders. A final sequence of purges had driven him to England, a country his mother had often described in glowing terms, where he hoped to forget the horrors of the past and if possible start life afresh.

No one knew very much about his sufferings; but it was understood, from hearsay, that his parents died about that time. Lady Goodfellow hinted that they had both been executed for political reasons, but that was mere guesswork, based on vague allusions and in no way supported by detailed evidence. She realized his aversion to talking about his past life and was therefore careful not to question him too closely. Besides, it was no concern of hers. The thing that mattered to her, which she extolled as no one else could and which never failed to draw the warmest admiration from even the most reactionary audience, was the way in which this down-and-out exile had managed to rally against the blows of fate and to command respect in the highest circles of a foreign country by acquiring, in a few years, a leading position in English literature. It was also the way in which he had adopted the language, the customs, even the mental outlook of his new surroundings; his affection for the country of his choice, which was evident in everything he wrote; and the gratitude he felt toward it. Finally, it was his gallantry as a front-line soldier during the campaign in France.

Conrad's rapid success was due to genuine talent and personal experience of a wide range of subjects. In his youth, he said, he had traveled all over the world in connection with his father's business concerns. Perhaps he had also been helped at the outset of his career by the similarity between his own name and that of a celebrated writer who, like himself, was of Polish origin and had likewise adopted English as his language and assumed British nationality. This predecessor may have saved him from the distrust to which any unprecedented action usually gives rise.

His novels bore the stamp of a vivid imagination and a cultivated mind. The public had given his first book an enthusiastic reception, and from then on his future was assured. But he had gradually begun to look on novel writing as a rather frivolous relaxation from what he believed to be his really important work. Conrad had forecast the war long before it was declared. His journeys in Europe, particularly in the new Germany he hated, had left no doubt in his mind. Under the pressure of

German rearmament he had directed his talents into one specific channel: He had assigned himself the task of warning his new compatriots against the Nazi menace and opening their eyes to the danger of living in a fool's paradise. In 1937 he had written, for an influential newspaper, a series of articles denouncing Nazi fanaticism. Through their obvious authenticity and unquestionable logic, they had attracted some attention in Government circles, though without quite achieving their purpose. The politicians read him. They agreed with what he said. But none of them did anything about it. . . .

At this point in her narrative, Lady Goodfellow raised her lovely eyes heavenward, as though to convey the heights of ministerial inefficiency. Sir Wallace made no comment.

In the beginning, the war had disrupted Conrad's career as a journalist and writer. When the storm he had so clearly foreseen actually broke, he refrained from blaming anyone and was therefore all the more admired. Instead, he joined up in the British army. His success, his influential friends, and the proof he had given of his loyalty had, a few months earlier, yielded the blessing of British nationality. An assignment to an Officer Cadets Training Unit was the first privilege he applied for in his new national status. This noble action was warmly applauded, and the last traces of suspicion due to his "funny foreign accent" were wiped out once and for all.

He was then thirty-three years old. He was sent to the O.C.T.U. at W———, and it was there that he met Patton—Arthur Patton, a philosophy don—who had likewise given up his job to fight for freedom. Both men quickly adapted themselves to their new profession and a few months later were graduated together with the rank of second lieutenant. Then they were shipped overseas, where they distinguished themselves in several skirmishes during the period of the phony war.

At the time of the full-scale German advance in 1940, Conrad was a captain and had won the M.C. Pinned down with the rest of his unit in a village in Flanders, he had held out till the last hand grenade, then succeeded in escaping with what remained of his men. Completely cut off from his headquarters, he managed, after some desperate hand-to-hand fighting, to seize an enemy ammunition dump; then, reinforcing his company with the stragglers he picked up on the road, he helped cover the withdrawal to Dunkirk. Finally, after being badly wounded in the leg, he was sent home to England.

As his wife came to the end of this part of the story, Sir Wallace broke in to explain that Conrad owed his life to the devotion of his men, who worshiped him; they had carried him back against his will.

He spent three months in a hospital on the outskirts of London. It was there that he first met Lady Goodfellow, who used to visit the casualties. With her naturally tender feelings and romantic inclinations, in which there was also a slight trace of insular snobbery, she could not fail to be attracted by this hero, a celebrated writer, whose foreign background invested him with an aura of mystery and glamour. She was soon completely enchanted by his fine intelligence and modesty and by the quixotic side of his character, and went out of her way to make his convalescence more bearable. There sprang up between them a deep affection, a friendship that had since remained strictly platonic.

While in the hospital Conrad had received a letter from Patton, whom he had last seen during the retreat, saying that he had also made good his escape and was at that moment on the south coast recovering from a slight wound. A few days later his friend came to see him. They spent the afternoon talking about their various adventures and making plans for the future. For the philosophy don the future was clear. At the end of his fortnight's leave, which he had devoted to copying out and bringing up to date the diary he had kept since joining up, he was probably going to be sent to the Middle East. He was thrilled by the thought of traveling farther afield and by the idea of taking part in those tank maneuvers in the middle of the desert that were then beginning to be widely discussed. That at least had been his initial plan. But for the last few days an even more attractive prospect had captured his imagination. There was yet another opportunity for exploiting the war so as to broaden his own personal experience. A clash with Japan was inevitable. A small force was being sent out to Burma, Malaya, and Hong Kong. They were asking for volunteers. "The East, you know," he solemnly explained. Patton's main concern was to broaden the scope of his knowledge by accepting this offer of excitement that miraculously coincided with his sense of duty. Conrad fully understood his attitude. There was nothing he could say, for he understood from the way his friend had said "The East" that his mind was already made up.

For himself the future was not so simple, for reasons that were unknown even to his closest friends.

Unaware of these reasons, Lady Goodfellow could therefore only outline the salient events in his life. She knew these events from what he had told her about himself, and all the better for having herself played a minor role in some of them. That at least was what she liked to think. Shortly before his discharge from the hospital, Conrad had been visited by Gordon, managing editor of *Victory,* an old friend of his. *Victory* was the paper for which Conrad had worked before the war, when his widely read articles had doubled its circulation.

T. H. Gordon did not make a habit of visiting the sick and wounded. He had other things to do. He had come because he had something to say, and he said it without wasting words. He began by asking Conrad what his plans were. Conrad replied that the state of his leg would not allow him to resume active service for several months and that meanwhile he was going to apply either for a post as interpreter to the Polish troops in Britain or else for a staff appointment.

Gordon then announced that never in the whole of his long career had he ever set eyes on such a silly pig-headed ass. He had said nothing when, at the outbreak of the war, Conrad had dropped him like an old shoe and had gone off to play soldier on the Continent; he had said nothing because he knew it would be useless. But if Conrad still insisted on turning down a really important assignment; if, on the ridiculous pretext of belonging to a so-called combatant unit, a writer of his standing was content to chain himself to a desk in order to copy out orders any little fool in the regular army could scribble down just as efficiently; then all he, T. H. Gordon, could do, now that his best lead writer had abandoned him, was to pin a large notice on the door of the *Victory* office, join up as a private in order to polish the boots of some idiotic general, and send all the bigwigs who had entrusted him with this damned propaganda mission to the devil.

Being used to these outbursts, C
Gordon out, then asked him to exp
about. Gordon did so, lowering hi
over the patient's bed in a mysteri
complete contrast to his normal ja

"Our propaganda system, my bo
it shouldn't be. Everybody knows it. The Minister himself agrees. He knows it's deplorable, but he hasn't a single competent assistant to reorganize his department. In this particular field the Germans are streets ahead of us. The morale of this country isn't as high as it seems. Goebbels' lies have been well received in certain circles, and there's a group of people so scared by the power of the Reich that they'd welcome peace at any price. It's a small group, I know, but it does exist. We can't let things go on as they are. The Minister, for once, has decided to take action. He has asked me to launch a systematic campaign in the paper, in terms the general public will understand but something substantial instead of the usual drivel. There's no point in describing how, single-handed, some gallant Tommy captured a dozen hulking great Huns petrified with fear round three machine guns and, whistling 'Tipperary,' brought them back to our lines. The Government wants something more convincing, not just fairy stories. I ought to explain that this *Victory* campaign is merely the first part of a far larger overall scheme that will make its effect felt later on. The Minister only gave me a rough outline. Finally, I ought to tell you that the only reason for his approaching me, T. H. Gordon—an old fool as far as military matters are concerned, who couldn't tell the difference between an armored car and a combine—the only reason is that through me he hoped

you, you, William Conrad, whose prose was ... served up at the breakfast table of every ...able household in London. What's more, I told ...n that I would only take on the job if you came back to us. That's all. Now it's up to you."

Conrad had asked for a week to think it over. He had consulted his doctors. They had told him his leg would need medical attention for another year at least. He had also sought the advice of Lady Goodfellow, who visited him as regularly as ever and had become something of a confidante. There was no doubt in his mind that it was she who had first thought of this new job for him and had asked her husband to arrange it. He had examined his conscience. Finally, he had considered those factors that have already been mentioned, which were known to no one but himself. At the end of the week he had accepted.

As soon as he was demobilized, he rejoined the *Victory* staff, and in a few weeks the paper's circulation exceeded even Gordon's sanguine expectations. Lady Goodfellow secretly hoped that in taking this decision he had been swayed by the prospect of staying on in London and occupying a place of honor among the elect who were invited to her weekly dinner parties.

Conrad skirted the damp grass of Green Park, walked down the arcade of the Ritz, and left the gloom of Piccadilly to turn off into the almost total darkness of the side streets. He eventually reached his destination and made his way to the office that Gordon had set aside for his exclusive use. The other journalists worked in a communal room and typed their copy themselves. He had a cubbyhole of his own, separated by a partition from the Managing Editor's. Miss Barker, Gordon's private secretary, worked for him as well.

His article was there, already typed out. It needed only correcting and signing. Next to it Miss Barker had carefully put out two letters for him that had arrived by the evening mail. The first bore a Far East B.A.P.O. stamp—it was obviously from Patton. Patton had not been able to resist the lure of the East. Conrad opened the letter and ran through it quickly. It was out of date, written before the Japanese invasion, and had arrived by a roundabout route. In the letter Patton described his first impressions of Malaya. Conrad put it in his pocket, intending to read it at his leisure when he got home.

The second letter came from a large town in the north. Conrad was surprised, for he knew nobody in that part of the country. It was from an anonymous admirer and consisted of several pages of gushing compliments. After a rapid glance Conrad was about to put it back on his desk when a certain word caught his eye. He studied it more closely, and his attitude suddenly changed. He put the letter in his billfold and hurriedly signed his article without rereading it.

He called for Miss Barker. She was waiting in the room next door, hoping to heaven that he would not keep her too long. He handed her the sheets of copy and absent-mindedly muttered, "Here, Joan. It's ready. You can send it down."

The girl could not believe her luck, for although she found Conrad easy to work for, she also knew he had a passion for last-minute revisions and would never overlook a typing mistake or even a misplaced comma. Her surprise got the better of her common sense.

"No corrections, sir?" she exclaimed.

But Conrad was already out of the room. From the landing he shouted back, "No, no, it's all right," then dashed down the stairs and went out to try and find a taxi.

He lived in a small flat near the Embankment. The journey there seemed interminable. He paid the driver, giving him a few extra coins without noticing the tip came to more than the fare itself. He scarcely answered when Mr. Malone, the hall porter, called out, "Good night, sir," but went past his desk almost at a run. The elevator was out of order. He went up the five flights without giving a thought to his leg. As soon as he was inside his flat, he carefully locked and bolted the front door. He lived alone; only Mrs. Malone came in to do the housework every morning. He made sure his curtains were drawn and that no one could see into the room. Then he sat down at a little writing desk, took the letter out of his billfold, and examined it again.

"Not a shadow of doubt," he muttered.

He got up, went over to the bookshelf, and took down a heavy volume. It was the 1924 edition of the *Pocket Oxford Dictionary*. He put it on the desk, next to the letter, and embarked on an all-absorbing task.

It was midnight. After listening to a recapitulation, in detail, of the merits of William Conrad, the Goodfellows' guests had once again discussed the disaster. The end of the evening had been most depressing, and Colonel Field had not even tried to conceal his feelings about the absence of "the right men in the right places" in Government circles. The guests had left on a note of despondency.

Lady Goodfellow said good night to her husband and

went off to pray for better news in the morning and get ready for bed. The couple slept in separate rooms. This enabled Sir Wallace to indulge in his little nightly debauch, which was harmless enough, though his wife would not have tolerated it for a moment. After putting on a gorgeous dressing gown, relic of the good old days, the Chairman of the National Recovery League opened a cupboard and from a locked drawer to which he alone had the key took out a half-empty bottle of John Haig. He then disappeared into the bathroom, came back with a carefully rinsed drinking glass, and poured himself an ample measure. This he began to drink in deep gulps. His features softened, and his face lost the graveyard expression the news of the sinking had stamped on it. His thoughts turned once again to the loss of the ship, and he decided it called for another drink. The whisky had been bought in great secret on the black market through the agency of a canny friend of his from Scotland. This was the only departure from the rules of austerity the old baronet allowed himself; and even then it caused him a twinge of conscience, which was only relieved by the fine quality of the Scotch. As he rolled heavily into bed, he felt there was certainly something in what Colonel Field had said about not having the right men in the right places. This forthright statement put him in mind of the talents of William Conrad. He once more went over the salient features of Conrad's brilliant career, and this mental review gave him sufficient food for thought until he fell asleep.

Lady Goodfellow was brushing her hair before going to bed. The loss of the *Prince of Wales* did not fill her thoughts as much as her usual daydream, which centered in William Conrad. She was not in love with him—on that score, again, a foreigner might have made a rash judgment; she simply placed him on a pedestal and invested him with the triple crown of genius, gallantry, and glamour. Sir Wallace could therefore sleep undisturbed after finishing his second glass of whisky. She would have smilingly discouraged any amorous approach more daring than a simple kiss; and William Conrad, who respected her for this, never asked her for anything more than affection.

It was midnight. Having contributed her quota to the national effort by a hard day's work, Miss Barker had gone off to see her boy friend, who was waiting for her at a Paddington hotel. The loss of her virginity to a member of the armed forces and longer working hours had been the main consequences of the war as far as she was concerned. These two factors were connected in her mind with a noble sense of patriotic duty. Her boy friend was a flight-lieutenant who had been wounded during one of the first sorties in the war and was now working in the Air Ministry. As she came in, he gave her a kiss and a bar of chocolate he had saved from his candy ration. They were both looking forward to spending the whole night together—a stroke of luck that did not often come their way. Usually, she had to stay on in the office till two or three o'clock in the morning; he had to be on duty at seven. She told him that her unexpected respite was due to Gordon's absence and to an inexplicable departure from habit on the part of her other boss. The flight-lieutenant said he only wished it happened more often and denounced the habits of journalists in general and William Conrad in particular. But Miss Barker, who, like everyone else, cherished a secret glow of admiration for that great man, retorted that she would not hear a word against him, especially as he was doing such an important job. The flight-lieutenant said no more, and both of them then concentrated exclusively on making the most of their present good fortune.

It was midnight in London, seven o'clock in the morning in the Malay Peninsula. At Singapore a few young naval officers, survivors from the *Prince of Wales,* were preparing to go on duty, looking rather hangdog after spending the whole night drowning their sorrows. With its usual consideration for "the human element," Headquarters had turned a blind eye on this understandable debauch. The Royal Navy had done the survivors proud. They had each received a grant of £200 to compensate for the loss of their personal kit, an official gesture that led a young midshipman to declare that at this rate he would not mind being torpedoed and sunk every day.

A few hundred miles farther north, between Penang and Kuala Lumpur under the gleaming palm trees of a Malayan kampong, Patton's company was recovering its breath after a long all-night withdrawal. The only aircraft overhead had Japanese markings. "What has happened to the bloody air cover?" Patton's Highlanders kept asking in amazement. He tried to reassure them by explaining that the Australian squadrons were probably being held in reserve for the moment. They would turn up at the proper time, when the Jap convoys had been sent to the bottom and their ground troops cut off on the peninsula with all their lines of communication broken. The news of the *Prince of Wales,* which had put London into mourning, had not yet reached the front line. Little news of any kind ever came through. Orders and counterorders, following in close and monotonous succession, bore evidence of a total administrative breakdown. Patton remembered Dunkirk, began drawing certain comparisons, and between a couple of bursts of machine-gun fire, his thoughts turned to William Conrad. It was a long time since he had heard from him. And he himself had not had a spare moment to write since coming up north. He made up his mind to drop Conrad another line at the first opportunity. If there was ever a man who would be in his element in this particular scrap, where no one knew what was happening, that man was William Conrad, the dashing man of action who could always adapt himself to the most unlikely situations.

It was two o'clock in the morning. Sir Wallace was at work in a place unknown to his ordinary acquaintances, his more intimate friends, and even his wife. It looked like a commonplace office, not unlike that of the usual businessman. The brass plate on the door specified that the business was that of a real-estate agent. Sir Wallace had slept only one hour; then he had arisen and dressed, unnoticed by Lady Goodfellow, and had left his home, ultimately to arrive at this rather unparliamentary office.

Here Sir Wallace did not drink. Sir Wallace was not concerned with the recovery of scrap material. Sir Wallace was thinking. Here, nearly every night, he spent some time deep in thought, thought which sometimes led to decisions of great consequence. That night he was again thinking of William Conrad, but with a different mind, and his frown of concentration showed the importance he attached to that particular person.

3

In the outwardly quite ordinary letter from an unknown admirer Conrad had noticed three small peculiarities: The sentence at the end of the second paragraph was in brackets, and this sentence was of exactly seven words. The third line of the letter began with the word "admirable." And lower down there was a word, standing just before an irregular verb, that was crossed out. None of these details was particularly significant in itself. All over the world, no doubt, and every day of the year, there were dozens of perfectly innocuous letters delivered that contained either a sentence of seven words in brackets, or the word "admirable" at the beginning of the third line, or an illegible word standing just before an irregular verb. But the presence of all three factors in a single letter had been enough to make Conrad neglect his duties as a journalist.

He worked away feverishly. He had not wasted much time on reading the writer's handsome compliments. He had simply picked out a number of words—chosen, it seemed, at random—and had written them down one after the other on a sheet of paper. An incongruous assortment of verbs, adjectives, nouns, and prepositions had been marshaled in the process. He then looked up each of these words in the 1924 edition of the *Pocket Oxford Dictionary* and carefully noted the numerals that made up the number of the page on which they appeared. He then went back to a particular passage in the same reference book and correlated every figure he had just obtained to a specific letter in that passage by means of a fairly simple transposition system. These letters made up certain words; and these words, when strung together, had a definite meaning. Conrad read them over under his breath and remained deep in thought.

He took out his lighter, set fire to the sheet of paper, the letter, and the envelope, made sure that all three were destroyed, then ground the ashes to powder. He put back the dictionary, lit a cigarette, and sank into a massive leather armchair, the only luxurious piece of furniture in the room. He recalled certain incidents that had happened in the past, that past of his which Lady Goodfellow knew nothing about.

William Conrad was not a Pole. It was true that his family came from Danzig and that he had lived there himself until an iniquitous treaty, a *Diktat* imposed by a brutal enemy, had severed it from the great Reich; but a stroke of the pen, the handiwork of bungling legislators, could not change the character of the people. His mother was a typical *Frau,* with eyes of Wedgwood blue and corn-colored hair. His father was a Prussian officer who had been killed in action. In his veins flowed the blood that Adolf Hitler praised for its purity and which, he claimed, could be traced back to the days when the Nordic gods fathered the first Aryan tribe. The type of man Conrad had passed himself off as in London society, in the army, and in literary circles had been created by himself, bit by bit, in accordance with certain directives he had received from a foreign service shrouded in mystery.

William Conrad was eight years old in 1914. He grew up in the shadow of war, in the fiercely patriotic atmosphere of his immediate surroundings. The impression these left on him at that time determined his subsequent career.

He seldom saw his father out of uniform, that German officer's uniform that was associated in his mind with supermen; and every night he went to sleep with his head full of the tales of heroism that made the infrequent visits of this demigod all the more memorable. He was descended from a long line of military men who had for generations distinguished themselves by the sword. Much blood had been shed in his family for the glory of victorious Prussia. Military prowess and the science of arms were considered the cardinal virtues, and between battles the memory of past exploits was venerated with almost religious solemnity.

Relatives too old to take an active part in the epoch-making campaigns of the First World War used to discuss the reports from the front in tones of rapture. The women set an example of patriotic fervor that seemed to combine, in a single mystic fusion, the qualities of valor, self-sacrifice, and devotion to the Fatherland. Conrad's mother subscribed to this tradition. While her husband was away covering himself with glory, she brought her son up on the family creed. Every evening she made him pray to the great Teuton god to lead the German army to victory. She would have thought it a sin to say a special prayer for her husband. When he was killed, she choked back her tears and exploited his death as a lesson in fortitude for the benefit of her son.

It was only in the hour of defeat that she finally gave way to her feelings. That day she clasped her son to her breast and took him into the room she had turned into a sort of shrine adorned with her heroic husband's arms and decorations. There, with the knell of defeat tolling in their ears, she made her son swear to devote his life to exacting vengeance.

This scene had left its mark on Conrad's tender susceptibilities. At the magnitude of the task before him he felt a shiver of excitement run through him; and even at that age, with the vivid imagination that was later so evident in his character, he felt, in the midst of his grief, a thrill of pleasure, the pleasure he anticipated at the prospect of avenging the Fatherland.

The thought of that future bliss enabled him to endure every hardship. His mother decided to leave the martyred city that was now being run by a hateful international league, and with great difficulty succeeded in reaching Berlin with her memories, her son, and her pride intact. She felt no pang at leaving behind most of her worldly goods. Without the moral standards to which she had been accustomed, she felt lost and preferred a life of drudgery to the shame of bondage. She took a humble job and devoted all her spare time to turning her son's heart to stone, at the same time anxiously observing the development of his physical strength.

The only possible career for him was the army. But he had to wait a long time before achieving his ambition. The army, reduced to a mere police force by the spiteful enemy, was in no need of recruits. He learned to be patient in the hope that one day these indignities would come to an end and that revenge would taste all the sweeter for having been so dear. Meanwhile, as an outlet for his energy, he steeped himself in the history of his country and the events that had contributed to her glory: the lives of her leaders, the accounts of her military campaigns, her literature, philosophy, and thought.

More advanced for his age than his contemporaries, in spite of his mother's efforts to keep him on the narrow path of manly virtues, and impelled by some instinct he himself could not explain, he felt he ought not to overlook a single aspect of the Fatherland's greatness. During the disruption of all education that followed the defeat and the revolution, he himself drew up as his curriculum a complete investigation into every element that had contributed to the formation of the German mentality. He learned, understood, and retained what he had learned with a facility that could only be explained by the constant ferment he was in. He read voraciously. He was so disposed by nature and upbringing that his brain worked just as well in a fever of excitement as in the mellower mood of critical analysis. His idealism did not conflict with his sense of reality. The one merely served to complement the other.

His interests gradually became more and more esoteric. He was fascinated by the dawn of German literature. Medieval legends provided him with model heroes who fulfilled all the requirements of his youthful imagination, and he learned long passages of the *Nibelung-*

enlied by heart. Klopstock, Lessing, and von Herder he regarded as the very essence of the German soul, the forerunners of the masterpieces of German literature. He liked Goethe, though he did not think he had any specifically Teuton quality and he found his humanism rather lacking in vitality. For some time, and almost in spite of himself, he was captivated by Heine. Then he tackled the great philosophers of the romantic period with the same fervor with which he had studied the poets. At the age of sixteen he was able to absorb and assimilate the most difficult texts. He steeped himself in the dry meditations of Kant, and even Hegel held no terrors for him. He recognized in Hegel's work the birth of an entity superior to the individual and far more complex, an organism to which every other element was subordinate; to Conrad's mind that organism was the German nation. In his imagination he saw this new being as a concrete materialization—the embodiment, according to his way of thinking, of all those supreme virtues he had set himself to acquire.

Nietzsche, he felt, provided him with a more immediate and accessible ideal in the highly colored image of the superman, to which he felt himself irresistibly drawn. Nietzsche also gave him sufficient reason for believing in the virtue of this ideal and in the merits of divine wrath. When he felt he had thoroughly digested the works of this philosopher, he conscientiously compared himself with the model described and tried wherever possible to reduce the differences he found by systematically ridding his mind of every feeling of tenderness. He could not bear the idea of groveling among a lot of lesser men. He came across certain passages that seemed to have been written exclusively for himself:

"I test the power of a will according to the amount of resistance it can offer and the amount of pain and torture it can endure by knowing how to turn that pain and torture to its own advantage."

Conrad shivered with excitement at these words and felt he had doubled in stature by virtue of the holy martyrdom he had suffered since the defeat.

He did not limit his academic ventures to the frontiers of his own small world. These provided the focal point for his investigations, but he was not averse to searching still farther afield. He devoted himself particularly to the study of languages, especially those of the hateful nations who were trying to stifle the energies of the young Reich. It was a period of solitary indoctrination, divided among work, meditation, and daydream.

Conrad did not have a single real friend. His contemporaries were either waiting for the hour of revenge without doing anything to bring it any nearer or else had accepted defeat with a resignation he despised. He still remembered how angry he had once been at a students' meeting, when he had heard one speaker attacking the spirit of militarism that had caused so much bloodshed and praising the policy of discretion that had put an end to the latest holocaust. He had not been able to control himself. He could think of nothing to say in answer to such shameful heresy, but in a paroxysm of rage sprang at the wretch's throat and buried his fist in his face. An irresistible force impelled him to pulverize those lips that had uttered such blasphemy. He did not let go until he had beaten the man to a pulp and almost strangled him in the bargain. After this incident he attended no more students' meetings and was only to be seen among a small group of young men who cherished the same ideals he did.

At long last a ray of hope pierced the darkness of his martyrdom. The National Socialist Party, the party of the workingman, proudly unfurled the flag that cowardly politicians had dragged in the mud. But how many indignities had been suffered in the meantime: the dismemberment of the Empire; an inhuman peace treaty whereby the severed pieces were partitioned among a lot of ruthless enemies; hateful troops once more invading German territory to exact the impossible payment of prohibitive reparations! It was then that the voice of the prophet had been heard for the first time, a single voice raised in anger against these iniquities and instilling in the people a sense of national importance. But patience was needed, still more patience. Instead of heeding and following the guide who showed them the path they should take, the masses tried to drown his voice and fondly believed that a prison cell would reduce him to silence.

But iron bars could not restrain him. In a short time the prophet became a godhead, a source of hope for those who had eyes to see. It took him ten years to scale the ladder leading from the soapbox to the seat of government, but long before he had reached those heights his initial supporters knew that he would provide the opportunity for revenge. Conrad had been one of those early supporters. In the fanatical speeches he seemed to hear the echo of his own conscience. The appearance of a new creed gave him a new lease on life. The few fresh ideas it expressed provided such a sop to his pride that he never noticed the inconsistencies of *Mein Kampf*. He questioned neither its premises nor its conclusions. He swallowed the whole doctrine in one mouthful: Germany had never been defeated on the field of battle; the country had been betrayed by the Jews; the Jews were responsible for its present plight. He realized more clearly than ever what a monstrous swindle the Treaty of Versailles had been. He was fully aware of the pure, sublime qualities of his race, the Teuton race, the master race, and looked forward to the splendid part it had been called upon to play in the future of the universe.

From then on, even before the Burning of the Books in 1933, Conrad purged his mind of all desire for literature that did not have as its basic theme the glorification of Germany. He tore up the works of Goethe and Heine, feeling almost like a criminal for having once had a taste for the poetry of the latter, that Jewboy who had had to go abroad to seek the recognition that had rightly been denied him by the truly chosen race. He confined his reading to the new literature, the literature known as "blood-and-earth" (Teuton blood and Teuton earth, of course) that a handful of zealous tyros were beginning to create round the central pillar of *Mein Kampf*. With this his intellectual development was complete. Now that he had reached the age of twenty, a rather more active service claimed his undivided attention.

He served at first in some paramilitary formations and finally in the army. He had a natural gift for the job, and his keenness and intelligence were the marvel of all his instructors. He wept with joy when he saw himself at last in officer's uniform.

But he had given such proof of devotion to the Nazi party that while the new leaders let him quietly serve his apprenticeship in arms they followed his career and earmarked him as a potential valuable asset. In 1930, when the demigod realized that supreme power was almost within reach, one of his apostles who had long before noticed the qualities of this particular young officer decided to offer him an opening in another direction. Conrad accepted without hesitation, delighted at having been specially selected. He had understood for some time from which quarter the true wind of nationalism was blowing.

He resigned from the army to become one of those anonymous agents who worked in the background for the glory of their country. The *Führer* recognized them as the units of a clandestine armada that was as indispensable to the realization of his scheme as regular troops in the field. Conrad developed a taste for this new profession in which his courage, education, and sense of responsibility had a chance of being put to the test. To begin with, he went through a special course lasting several months, in which he was taught the various subjects a secret agent had to master if he were to bring the strange missions he undertook to a successful conclusion. The course covered a wide range, including training in jujitsu and lectures on foreign politics. At the same time he perfected his knowledge of foreign languages, since it was in enemy territory that he was to be employed. He soon showed he had outstanding qualifications and gave ample evidence of his ability. As part of his training he was taken on trips to various parts of Europe; then, taking advantage of his knowledge of Polish, his superiors sent him on a tricky mission across the frontier into that country, where the German race was living under the constant duress of a heartless partition. He accomplished this mission so successfully that he was looked upon as a man of whom great things could be expected.

It was to Danzig, his birthplace, that he was sent to sow the seeds of unrest and prepare the fifth column for the advent of the new masters. There was nobody there who could recognize him, for he was then twenty-five years old. The dawn of a glorious future was breaking, and he felt the delirious joy of contributing to the realization of his dreams by doing a job that taxed his mental and physical resources to the full. The propaganda campaign he launched was so efficient, his networks so well organized, that two years later, only a few months after the *Führer's* absolute seizure of power, the town offered of its own accord to come under the protection of the demigod and his disciples. The police went over to the Nazis en masse. Storm troopers fought pitched battles in the streets. All that remained, once Rauschning was got rid of, was for Greiser to take up the reins of office.

Forster, the Nazi gauleiter, got all the official credit. The name of William Conrad was not mentioned. His business, he knew, was to avoid the limelight and remain unseen in the background. The only thanks he got was from his departmental chief. But that was more than enough; the satisfaction of a job well done was ample reward for his pains. He combined all the qualities that were needed to succeed in this arduous, thankless work, for which tact and ingenuity were as essential as brute force sometimes was. His education and natural intelligence had saved him from the many traps into which equally devoted but less experienced agents had fallen. His propaganda campaign had been a masterpiece of its kind. He knew instinctively what argument would appeal to each section of the community and could state his case with the exact degree of forcefulness and clarity that each of his audiences demanded. He knew when to make use of threats and when to wheedle, when to appeal to fear and when to reason. He could go on repeating himself indefinitely when he felt repetition was necessary; he was never at a loss for the right concrete example to illustrate an abstract idea; and he found no difficulty in investing the tritest sentiments with an aura of mysticism or in introducing the doctrines of the National Socialist Party in the guise of patriotic duty. He could also, when it suited his book, show utter ruthlessness, harden his heart against the sight of human misery, and sacrifice to the glory of the cause every individual interest, including his own. Had he not been forced by circumstance to remain in the background, he would have made a very great leader.

All this time he was so absorbed in his mission that his mother's illness and death hardly affected him at all. He used to stay with her for a day or two whenever he came back from his clandestine trips abroad to report to his chiefs on the progress achieved. But she did not live to see the dawn of the resurrection. Conrad had never told her what his job really was; in the interests of security he had had to make that sacrifice. As far as his friends were concerned, he was a journalist, a foreign correspondent; and to make this cover story sound more plausible, he had even had a series of purely descriptive articles published in a nonpolitical magazine. His mother never forgave him for leaving the army and betraying the memory of his ancestors, and she died of a broken heart and of bitterness pent up since the defeat. Conrad said a short prayer over her grave and under his breath renewed the vow he had made as a child; then he immediately reported back for duty. Compassion was not one of the virtues his religion demanded.

After his success at Danzig, he was singled out for another, more momentous assignment. He was told that a high-level decision had been taken to send him on a mission of the greatest possible importance deep into the heart of enemy territory: to England, in fact, perfidious England, haven of international Jewry and home of those malignant powers standing in the way of German resurrection. His preparations lasted two years, during which he systematically added to his knowledge of that country, its customs, and history, and also its literature and even its poetry, for he was eager to learn all he could about the weak points in the enemy's armor.

For the thousandth time he recalled the scene of his briefing for this mission. The head of the department had called him in one evening in great secrecy. With the chief was the man who had singled Conrad out at the very beginning of his career and who had since become one of the Party bigwigs. At a nod from this exalted person, the head of the department opened the conversation.

"A first-class man's needed in London, not for plain intelligence work—we're well provided in that direction—but for a really exceptionally important task that is not to take effect till much later and for which the necessary instructions will be issued when the time comes. The sort of man we want must be completely above suspicion and capable of contacting Government circles, winning the confidence of those circles, and exercising an influence in them. We've decided to send you off a few days from now. The papers you'll carry will provide you with a perfectly plausible identity—a political refugee from Poland. The rest's up to you. For the time being, don't forget, your main task is to inspire confidence. The usefulness of your subsequent activity will depend entirely on your achieving this initial objective. That activity is of such importance that in order to avoid the faintest shadow of suspicion being thrown on you we'll have to abstain more or less completely from communicating with you until the time is ripe. Meanwhile, concentrate on developing your assumed personality. Don't forget for a single second that you're a victim of Nazi persecution and one of its most ruthless opponents. You must pass yourself off as a loyal friend of England, a grateful friend, who will always stand up for the British way of life. In a few years' time we will be at war, but you're still to keep up the same appearances. When we think the time has come, we'll let you have further instructions." Then, turning to the high priest who had been silent all this time, the chief meekly inquired, "I don't think there's anything more to say, is there, sir?"

"No, that's all," the Party bigwig said. Then, turning to Conrad, "But I should like to stress once more how important it is for you to inspire confidence, to win it by every means at your disposal. You've been chosen for this job because with your education, experience, and adaptability you have more chance than most of bringing it off. Whatever happens, until further orders you're to behave like an Englishman. You're an Englishman at heart from now on, and don't forget it."

William Conrad had not forgotten. Realizing that an opportunity like this occurred only once in a lifetime, and conscious of his personal horizons perceptibly widening, he had marshaled every talent he possessed in the service of his new mission. In a few hours he had worked out a plan, according to the briefing he had been given, that enabled him to satisfy his lifelong ambition of creating a personality that would leave an indelible impression on the sands of time.

He had a sound knowledge of the English language, and in spite of himself appreciated its picturesque precision. He knew he had a flair for writing and was fairly confident of success in that direction. He knew, too, from the celebrated examples in the past, that foreigners could write masterpieces in English. To become a literary figure in enemy territory, and thereby come into contact with every section of the community, was the ideal means of fulfilling his mission. The English upper classes, in their blind snobbery, could not fail to be won over by a man of letters. In his arrogance he took no account of the difficulties, and his plan came off more easily than he had ever hoped. At the success of his first publication the joy he felt at having accomplished the initial part of his task was accompanied by a certain degree of personal satisfaction. Duty apart, he was proud of having succeeded in a profession to which he was naturally attracted.

With what growing impatience he had followed the triumphant rise to power of the Nazi party and its leader! The lying reports he read in the vile English press could not disguise the splendor of that resurgence. From the anxiety expressed in the newspapers he understood that the day of revenge was not far off, what with the *Führer's* reintroduction of conscription with a single stroke of the pen; his proud decision (published as an act of defiance) to create a *Wehrmacht* even mightier than the French army, and a *Luftwaffe* more powerful than the R.A.F.; his absolute determination to do away with the infamous *Diktat* of 1919; the occupation of the Rhineland; the full-scale rearmament, which the League of Nations condemned with a snivel but could do nothing to prevent; the provocative speeches of Goebbels inspiring the nation with a sense of ruthless self-sacrifice in view of the glorious future ahead ("Guns before Butter" ran the indignant headlines in *The Times*); the annexation of Austria; and finally the reconquest of Czechoslovakia and the pitiful show put up by the lily-livered Allies, who bowed their heads before the supreme will of the redresser of all these wrongs! At this rapid succession of events Conrad's devotion to duty reached fever pitch. His only anxiety was that the enemy might be too meek, too cowardly; that they would surrender without a fight; that his own role might be rendered superfluous by the sickening faintheartedness of these pacifists.

But he still had to animate the puppet that was his own handiwork, to pull the strings of the marionette he had created to suit British tastes. It was not without regret that, with the war clouds gathering, he had abandoned his purely imaginative work to devote himself almost exclusively to a farseeing and realistic propaganda system. He realized, however, that he had to make a move in this direction in order to confirm his reputation for loyalty and at the same time be in the political swim. Nor was it without a deep feeling of disgust that he had launched a series of violent attacks against "the enemy" and his religion. But he had been able to meet the cruel demands of duty, and after a short time had managed to get over his nausea. He enjoyed writing. When it came to stating a case so as to sway the masses, he was up to all the tricks, and he soon found a proper place for his talent in that direction. In its style and subject matter every article he wrote bore evidence of his singleness of purpose; and in this field of activity he even showed a vigorous command of language that was alien to his earlier works. In the freedom-loving press circles of London he gradually came to be regarded as a ruthless opponent of every form of tyranny and as a far-seeing prophet who never stopped declaiming against the dangers of Continental fascism. His masters had decreed what his attitude was to be. They had told him, "You're an Englishman at heart from now on, and you must convince everyone else that you are." All he had to do was to strengthen this conviction at every possible opportunity. This required less and less of an effort on his part, and there was no sign now of his initial awkwardness.

When war was declared, he had had to think twice. The only message he had received from his chiefs was to tell him to carry on as before and not do anything rash, since he would not be needed for at least another year. After thinking it over, volunteering for the army had seemed to him the perfect move to give the final touch of verisimilitude to the robot he had set in motion. After that gesture no one could have any doubt about him; and if the campaign abroad came to a speedy end with a wholesale withdrawal—and he had good reason to believe it would—a show of gallantry in action would break down the reservations of the few still a little in doubt about him. After that he would be certain to find some excuse for getting demobilized; or, better still, the authorities might insist on it, and then he would be able to resume his duties in absolute security.

He smiled as he thought how accurate his forecast had been. The memory of those days put him in mind of the O.C.T.U. at W——— and of his meeting with Arthur Patton. Suddenly he remembered the letter his old comrade-in-arms had sent him. He took it out of his pocket and read it over again.

4

This is what Patton had to say:

"My dear William,

"Here I am in Singapore. To be more precise, in a camp just north of it. I can't tell you much about the beauty of tropical forests, because so far I've seen only a few stunted trees on top of a hill near here, which have no doubt been kept there on purpose as part of the props for our instruction in jungle warfare. Under cover of this isolated clump we've been training every day since we arrived. I'm slowly improving and can now crawl through the grass in the approved manner, with a knife between my teeth and without making any noise so long as there are not too many mosquitoes about. This is the latest craze and has the official blessing of our most eminent strategists. You may laugh, but I'm enjoying it all immensely, and my only regret is that we don't move about a bit more. I'd like to see something of the interior, which everyone says is magnificent. Crawling on one's stomach through long grass limits one's field of view slightly.

"Everyone out here expects war to break out at any minute—with the exception, of course, of our government officials, who with their usual farsightedness say it's quite out of the question. But a native rag-and-bones man has just assured us it will happen any day now, so we're all in a dither of activity. Though the battle hasn't yet begun, I've already seen something of the enemy—in Singapore. Every photographer and barber in the place is a Jap. That's their monopoly. The Government in its loving kindness does nothing about them, so every morning our staff officers can be seen baring their lathered throats to the knives of these little yellow men. They're a pretty slick lot—the little yellow men, I mean.

"By now you must have got the letters I sent you on the way out, describing the voyage. From them you'll see that the Empire's in pretty good shape. The last lap took rather long because of some technical hitch in the engine room, so I had plenty of time to think about the Old Goat. The more I think about him, the more I'm convinced that even if his policy leads to disaster we've no right to laugh at his philosophical theories—we least of all, considering Bishop Berkeley and Samuel Butler, not to mention G.B.S. I firmly believe that if he had happened to be born in England he would have confined himself to theory and might have become a perfectly reasonable philosopher. His tragedy is that, being misunderstood by his own set, he's now trying to put theory into practice and is making an experimental test without taking any account of the time factor. Just think what would have happened if Darwin, in the space of a single generation, had done the same and tried to

create a vertebrate by throwing a handful of protozoic cells into a saucepan and then bringing the mixture to the boil! It would mean the end of the world. It's always a dangerous business when philosophers start doing things or when men of action dabble in ideas. But luckily we're still alive! All this, I'm sure, can be explained by environment and individual reaction. But I shan't go on because I know you don't agree and have always disapproved of my attempts to understand the Old Goat's psychological make-up. We'll have plenty of time when the war's over to discuss all this at our leisure.

"I can't think of anything more to say that could be of any interest to an old know-all like you. I go into town once or twice a week. The food's quite good. There's beer and Scotch to drink, and Chinese, Malayan, Javanese, and Indian girls to dance with—and sometimes even, in the smart clubs, white women as well. That's our life, and please don't hold it against us. I'm longing to hear from you and hope you're now completely recovered.

"Yours ever,

"Arthur Patton."

Conrad put the letter down. Even now that he was alone and had no need to hide his true feelings, he found he was not in the least annoyed by his friend's disparaging remarks. By the "Old Goat" Patton meant none other than the Chancellor himself, Adolf Hitler, in whom he had a professional interest.

He read the letter over again and was amazed. How on earth could an officer on active service with the British army be so frivolous about something so serious? How on earth did such lightly veiled insults against the civil and military authorities manage to get past the censors? It was almost a waste of time to bother about stratagems in order to deceive these people. Then his thoughts reverted once again to Arthur Patton.

One night when he was still in the O.C.T.U. training camp at W———, Conrad had been unable to sleep and had left the barracks to smoke a cigarette outside. He was thinking how odd it was to find himself a cadet in the British army when he heard a number of dull thuds, one after the other, like the noise of some heavy weight being dropped on the ground. He counted five thuds in succession, separated by an interval of a few seconds, then silence for several minutes. Then another series of five thuds; another long silence; and so it went on. The sound seemed to be coming from the sports ground, where the cadets, with the aid of a medicine ball, perfected their physical fitness.

After climbing over the hedge that hid the sports ground from view, Conrad stopped and listened again. During one of the long intervals of silence between two series of thuds, he saw a light flitting over the grass. After a moment it went out. Conrad drew nearer. He felt something whistle past him in the dark and heard it land beside him in the grass.

"What the devil—" he began to exclaim.

"What the devil yourself!" said a voice coming out of the shadows. "You can thank your lucky stars; you've only just missed having your head bashed in. Who is it, anyway?"

The flashlight went on again, and Conrad recognized a cadet who had arrived a few days before, Arthur Patton. His face was pouring with sweat, and in his hands were three unprimed grenades, which were used for practice.

"What the hell are you doing out here at this time of night?" Conrad asked him.

"Can't you see? I'm practicing throwing these damned things as far as possible. I'm not used to it, and with only a ten-minute training period during the day, I'll never get the hang of it. It needs a lot of practice, you know. You see, the grenade's used on patrols, mostly night patrols—at least, that's what they keep telling us—so that's why I'm putting in a little practice at nighttime. I throw five grenades one after the other, using that post over there on the sky line as a target. Then I go and pick them up and start all over again. Look, you've been here longer than I have; you must know more about it. Tell me, is this the correct stance?"

Patton got back into position and threw the three grenades he was holding one after the other, much to the amusement of Conrad, who watched him by the light of the flashlight.

"Well?" Patton asked when he had finished.

"Absolutely hopeless," said Conrad. "If you went on throwing live grenades like that, you might hit an enemy target one day—but not before killing off everyone in your own unit. That's not quite good enough, you know."

The healthy, carefree life of the camp and the companionship of the other cadets, who were almost all younger than he, sometimes led Conrad to adopt a slightly sarcastic tone that would have been out of place in the *Wehrmacht* but which he did not even try to conceal here, feeling that it was, if anything, an advantage. Patton was terribly upset.

"I knew there was something wrong. I'm always miles off the mark."

Conrad was moved by a sudden impulse to help him. "Look," he said, "hold the flashlight and watch how I do it."

And in the middle of the night, deep in the heart of the English countryside, he proudly gave this willing pupil a demonstration of his strength and skill. In his own country front-line soldiers and secret service agents were put through an exhaustive training course.

Thanks to Conrad, who soon became his closest friend, Patton eventually mastered the art of throwing grenades in all three positions—standing, lying, and kneeling. This young scholar, who was loaded with academic honors, set about studying military science with the same energy and concentration he devoted to every other field of learning, which endeared him all the more to William Conrad.

Arthur Patton, at the age of thirty-two, was a philosophy don in a provincial university, as he explained to his new friend one autumn morning when the two of them were on their way to breakfast together. When war was declared, he had only just finished a thesis that would have got him a better appointment and put him in the running for a professorship. Yet he had been one of the first to volunteer.

As though to justify his action, he explained, "In peacetime a philosopher's job is far more useful than most people think. But when there's a war on, you can't expect a philosopher to serve his country in that capacity. It's a different thing for engineers, doctors, chemists, and even mathematicians, whose jobs can quickly be adapted in the interests of national defense. But what earthly good is a philosophy don? That was a question I couldn't answer. Then I realized that the infantry was purposely created for people like me, who are of no practical use. Most of my colleagues felt the same way as I did and also joined up at once."

Conrad then told Patton who *he* was and was delighted to learn that his friend had read his books and liked them.

"You realize," Arthur Patton went on, "people like you and me have less to lose than anybody else in this show. We haven't had to give up any business or practice or any other job that might suffer by our being away; and, what's more, we're able to carry on with our own work, only in different surroundings, which gets us out of the routine rut. You can probably collect enough material for a dozen novels out of the life we're leading now, and I've got a far more varied field of study than any book can provide. Only the regulars are in as good a position as we are from the professional point of view. You're not married by any chance?"

"No," said Conrad.

"Neither am I. That would be the only fly in the ointment. As it is, everything's fine."

They had had to drop the subject at this point to go on parade; and while the Union Jack was hoisted to the masthead, the philosophy don and the secret service agent both presented arms, the one with elaborate care, the other with practiced ease, for it was some time since Conrad had been put off his stroke by the distant echo of words of command delivered in a rather more guttural language.

Conrad disengaged himself from his memories to devote a moment's thought to the present. He pictured Patton, hidden away in some corner of the jungle, on the lookout for an opportunity to apply his newly acquired crawling technique, being relentlessly machine-gunned by the Japanese air force yet showing no alarm at the present setbacks, remaining as firmly convinced as ever of the justice of the cause he was serving, constantly divided by his love of liberty, a passion for science, and infatuation with abstract problems, completely confident of the future of the Empire and utterly determined to bring about the ideal of "the greatest happiness of the greatest number," oblivious of the fact that the author of this admirable doctrine had been one of the fiercest opponents of British imperialism. What a mass of contradictions, thought Conrad, and what hypocrisy!

Yet he had not been able to resist Patton's companionship. Since his arrival in England he had made a number of friends in literary and society circles, but not one really close one. At what point, then, had his interest in this young don become a personal feeling, outside the scope of his official mission? He could not say for sure, any more than he could tell how far his close relationship with Lady Goodfellow was involuntary or intentional. But he did not even try to conceal from himself that this interest had gradually developed into a genuine attachment. This predicament came under the same heading as all those other unexpected situations created by the war. So he felt there was no need to lose any sleep over it.

He wondered whether Patton had taken his portable

bookcase with him. This thought plunged him once more into the past.

Every evening, when the afternoon lectures were over, after a shower and the inevitable cup of tea that betokened the end of another working day and boosted the morale of the flower of this sturdy nation, the cadets and the instructors at the O.C.T.U. training camp would get together in the "lounge." This was a recreation room in a barn that had been put at their disposal by a kindly administration with a fatherly eye on their welfare. There, at six o'clock every morning, teacher and pupil took each other on at darts.

His first night there Conrad had been approached by the Camp Commandant, a major with a handlebar mustache who was always on the lookout for a game. "Are you any good at the game?"

"I don't know, sir, I've never tried," he had answered.

He had subsequently learned how to play and had proved himself an adept.

The billiard table, evenly lit by three overhead lamps spaced at regular intervals, was the main attraction for the more serious-minded element. Every evening a team of instructors challenged a team of cadets to a match, and on the rare occasions when the latter won, the celebrations went on until late into the night.

At the far end of the room there were a few armchairs, grouped round a table littered with magazines. These, together with a cupboard lined with books provided by the local welfare organization, formed a refuge where the intellectuals could come and knit their brows. This was where Conrad ran into Patton the day after their first encounter, and it was here they subsequently met quite often for an evening's chat, in spite of the baleful glances of some of their colleagues whose nerves were frayed by the east wind and who had come there for a little peace and quiet.

Patton had brought with him a boxful of books, in which he used to bury himself, taking copious notes, as soon as he came off duty. He was forgiven this mild eccentricity, in the first place because he had a perfect right to do what he liked in his spare time, and secondly because he was always willing, if called upon, to handle a cue or throw a dart. He would enjoy these games as much as the keenest player, then wrap himself up once more in his reading. The subject he had chosen for his first thesis had been "The Origins of Thought," and it was now his ambition to write a sequel, on the evolution of thought and its relationship to matter. It was an immense undertaking, so immense, indeed, that, as Conrad pointed out, he might just as well think of tackling a universal exposition of every single phenomenon in the world. Patton blithely agreed that this was more or less what he was trying to do, for he planned to deal not only with Darwin's theory of natural selection but also with political upheavals and the petty everyday incidents of camp life.

The authorities he consulted were many and various. They included a good many learned commentaries on the origin of species and prehistory and on the gradual evolution or sudden mutations that had given birth to that masterpiece known as Homo sapiens. Natural science fascinated Patton almost as much as philosophy. But his book box also contained a number of other works. Conrad remembered the shock he had felt one evening when he found his friend absorbed in *Mein Kampf*.

This was not the first time Patton had taken him by surprise. A few days before he had treated him to a positive sermon on the German philosophers in general and Nietzsche in particular. Conrad had discreetly held his peace as he listened to his friend telling him there was certainly something to be said for the work of that great writer and that the theory of emergence was a ground on which the principle of free will could be reconciled to the basic laws of evolution. Its true significance, thank God, had been recognized by Samuel Butler and the neo-Lamarckians; no one in England was fettered any longer to the hopelessly mechanistic theories of Darwin. Conrad had controlled himself while Patton went on to say that the development of modern psychology had revealed positive traces of sexual repression in the philosopher's writing, which he himself had discerned in quite a number of his axioms; in any case, Nietzsche could never be completely forgiven for deriding John Stuart Mill, a man who was in every way his superior.

But seeing the bible of the National Socialist Party in the hands of a British officer-to-be, Conrad felt he should make some sort of protest. Arthur Patton quietly closed the book and launched with his usual gusto into the inevitable discussion thus provoked.

"You know, it's a great mistake to believe that any book is entirely negligible. Have you read *Mein Kampf*?"

"I had a look at it once. It's just a tissue of malicious lies and utter drivel."

"Now, now, keep your shirt on. I'm not trying to stand up for it. It's considered the most badly written and incoherent book that has appeared for a long time, and rightly so. The author's lack of balance is apparent on every page, and there's hardly a trace of logic or rational sequence of thought to be found from beginning to end. But don't forget, it's a propaganda tract written for the masses, and for the German masses, who are much more easily won over by arbitrary slogans than by properly drawn conclusions."

"Even so," Conrad blurted out, "I know a number of people among the so-called intelligentsia who think it's extremely sound."

"Really? How interesting! Do tell me about it, won't you? Any sort of firsthand experience like yours is of outstanding interest to me. Naturally, I can understand that after going through what you've been through on account of this particular ideology, it would be difficult to view it objectively. But personally I'm absolutely fascinated by Hitler, and I plan to do a long chapter on him."

So started William Conrad's torment. Patton broke into a lengthy monologue, in which he set out to analyze in the minutest detail everything the "Old Goat" had ever said or done, with a view to finding some reasonable explanation. And the fact that this analysis was wholly objective and betrayed the speaker's anxiety to remain completely impartial made it all the more unbearable. Patton felt there was something to be said for believing in the advent of the superman and of a master race, something that Nietzsche had only vaguely hinted at. The Nazi party had distorted and debased the idea by transferring it from the broad plane of all humanity to the narrow confines of a single nation, but it still could not, in all fairness, be disassociated from the philosophy of universal emergence, for which the young don had a deep respect. He explained to the luckless Conrad that to his way of thinking Hitler had started off by being a far greater idealist than his colleagues. The frequent allusions the *Führer* had made to biological development and natural laws showed a breadth of vision unknown in most politicians and a sense of evolution reminiscent of Professor Alexander's. These very genuine qualities had been nullified by the fact that none of his close associates was capable of living up to these aspirations. They had simply jeered at him. It was then that he developed a complex (Patton liked to think that all behavior was due to some complex or other). In his rage at being misunderstood, the "Old Goat" had insisted on demonstrating his principles, come what may, and had tried to create in a single generation what nature had not been able to achieve in a hundred thousand years. Patton concluded on a note of praise for the British wait-and-see policy, a much wiser policy than most people thought, based on the deep obligations Britain was called upon to fulfill. And finally, without denying the possibility or even the probability of future mutations in the direction of superhumanism, he still acknowledged the temporary necessity of a universal moral code, a code that had been summed up by Jeremy Bentham in a phrase that could scarcely be bettered: "The greatest happiness of the greatest number."

Conrad did not know what attitude to adopt and felt the greatest difficulty in keeping to his role. On the one hand, he had to pull the strings of his marionette and protest against such shocking impartiality; on the other, hearing his own theories on physico-biological phenomena being pulled to pieces in this manner made his blood boil so that he could hardly contain himself. He remembered just in time that he was living in the only country in the world where everyone had the inalienable right to voice his opinion without being interrupted until he had finished, and where tradition demanded that even then some time should be allowed to pass before any objection could possibly be raised—especially if the opinion expressed happened to be in the nature of a paradox. This gave him time to pull himself together. Having mastered his feelings, he entirely agreed with Patton about British policy, but with calculated fury inveighed against his overgenerous opinion of the *Führer's* personality. That pseudophilosophy of his, with its wretched scientific pretentiousness, was nothing but false romanticism arising from a little learning but insufficient knowledge. Patton heard him out in silence but stuck to his own point of view, which he proceeded to back up by quoting several statements delivered by journalists and politicians after an interview with the Chancellor. Conrad ransacked his memory for some suitable instance to illustrate his master's mediocrity but could not think of anything sufficiently convincing or to his liking. He made up his mind to examine the ground more thoroughly so as not to be caught off guard next time. Meanwhile neither he nor Patton yielded an inch.

As time went on, Conrad gradually got used to the atmosphere of these discussions. Occasionally, just for fun, he would even start one himself and follow it up with carefully considered objections, put forward for the sole pleasure of hearing his friend give vent to yet another stream of paradoxes.

Patton's companionship introduced a welcome change into the normal pattern of camp life. Until then Conrad had looked upon the course as an unavoidable fatigue, enlivened only by the sardonic amusement he felt at the training methods. After the instruction he had received in the German army, he could not help smiling rather condescendingly at the military theories propounded by the officers of His Majesty's forces. He was sometimes bored to tears at having to listen to long-winded explanations of some point that to him was self-evident, and during field exercises he could scarcely conceal his impatience at the slowness and clumsiness of the tactics, when usually all that was needed to solve the problem was a little decision, resolute action, and a certain sacrifice of man power. He tried to picture an encounter between these backward amateurs and the fighting units he had known, which were trained for battle in their infancy. It would be a massacre, a parody of war. He felt no pleasure at the thought; in fact, he resented this inefficiency, for an easy victory would be a less glorious one.

He did his best not to reveal his own ability, but the little he did display enabled him to win an overwhelming ascendancy over his colleagues and a flattering report from his superior officers. Toward the end of the course, an Indian Army colonel delivered a series of three lectures on the principles of higher strategy and the tactical employment of large formations in the field. At the end of the last lecture, following the usual practice of British instructors, he asked whether there were any questions. Conrad got up, asked for permission to speak, and showed by his remarks that he had thoroughly digested the subjects under discussion. Carried away by his own enthusiasm, he started laying down the law to the lecturer himself and had no difficulty in demonstrating the weakness of some of his out-of-date theories. He submitted, as though he had just thought of them himself, a number of alternative suggestions based on Prussian training methods. In doing so he had acted quite involuntarily, moved only by the desire to see truth and reason triumph. (Later on, in the front line in France, he was moved by the same impulse to prove himself superior in courage and ability by treating these pacifists to a lesson in the real art of warfare.) The old Colonel was deeply impressed and was the first to admit there was something in what he said. When the lecture was over, he rushed off to the Orderly Room, took out his notebook, and for his own benefit carefully jotted down all the suggestions William Conrad had put forward, following them with the comment, "extremely interesting." Then he asked for the cadet's personal file, to which he appended a few words of praise, underlined in red ink.

These fellows will never learn, thought Conrad as he got into bed. He found himself now always thinking in English. They're still back in the days of trench warfare. It's not going to be much fun for us.

But on that score, for all his usual perspicacity, William Conrad was much mistaken. "These fellows" were eager to learn and were indeed learning. But their process of mental digestion was slow and their assimilation of ideas laborious. They did not overlook a single opening for furthering their knowledge. They were as familiar with the deductive method of reasoning as with the inductive, and the latter was particularly popular with them. It was true they had started off in 1939 with principles of warfare dating back to 1914. These were reliable, consistent principles that had been put to the test in the past. But no subsequent experience had been neglected, neither Lawrence's campaign in Arabia nor Weygand's strategy at the head of the Polish troops, nor Mussolini's conquest of Abyssinia, nor the Spanish Civil War.

Two years after war was declared, in the winter of 1941, a special commission consisting of senior officers had made a detailed study of the fighting in Spain and had come to certain conclusions about the technique of guerrilla warfare. As a result, Arthur Patton and a number of other young gentlemen in various parts of the Empire were learning to crawl on their stomachs with a knife between their teeth and slit the throats of enemy sentries. The special commission was still working twenty-four hours a day. The war between China and Japan was under review, and there would soon be further useful conclusions drawn from the invasion of Poland and the evacuation from Dunkirk.

PART TWO

5

The day after Lady Goodfellow's dinner party, Conrad got up earlier than usual, feeling relieved by the message from his chiefs and delighted to have heard from his friend. He answered Patton's letter, then went off to work.

The office was deserted. The busy time was the evening. Gordon usually never came in till after lunch; Miss Barker not before eleven o'clock, unless there was something special on. Conrad got down to work on his new article. The pleasure he found in this activity and the energy he devoted to it helped to dispel his pensive mood of the previous evening. Action was what he needed, and for the moment action consisted of making a name for himself by exploiting his natural talents and ingenuity.

He had already worked out the main features of his article. The Propaganda Minister, through Gordon, had suggested the subject: a general summary from which an obvious conclusion could be drawn. Conrad therefore proposed to trace the major political and military issues since the outbreak of hostilities, examine the causes of each Allied reverse, and point out the lesson to be drawn from them, ending with an outline of the present situation designed to show there were good grounds for a feeling of optimism.

He wrote quickly, making very few corrections. There were any number of arguments in favor of an attitude of confidence, and he put them forward with practiced ease. He drew a highly colored picture of the savage onslaught of 1940, giving a detailed technical account of the strategy, strength, and armament of the enemy at that time. He showed how heavily the Allies were outnumbered, giving this as the main reason for their defeat and drawing attention to the insignificance of the Belgian army, the unpreparedness of the French, and the paucity of the British Expeditionary Force. "Everything, in fact," he explained, "was in favor of the highly trained aggressor, whose success was far less due to his prowess in the field than to our own inferiority in numbers. The very fact that he has been unable to turn this advantage into a decisive victory shows how very far he is from perfection. Fighting under such hopeless conditions, our own troops gave a good account of themselves, proving beyond any doubt that they are quite capable of beating the much-vaunted German army as soon as they meet it on equal terms.

"Yet it is this very element of warfare—the employment of ground forces—that is our weakest point!"

He went on to deal with the evacuation from Dunkirk. He involuntarily let his enthusiasm run away with him as he recalled the splendid part played by the Royal Navy, which had performed this "miracle of deliverance," as Churchill had described it, this unimaginable feat of carrying "over 335,000 men, French and British, out of the jaws of death and shame, to their native land and to the tasks which lie immediately ahead." The rigid Prussian principles of warfare had been powerless to prevent this escape—startling proof, if proof were needed, of the endless resources of the Royal Navy, and symbol of the incontestable supremacy of Britain at sea.

Conrad went over the last sentences carefully. Realizing he had let himself be carried away by the music of the language and was therefore not being quite objective, he crossed out the phrases he felt were overfanciful and replaced them with factual details that would carry more weight with a serious-minded public.

"The Royal Air Force—" He was interrupted by the entry of Miss Barker, who had come through his office in order to reach the Managing Editor's.

"Good morning, sir," said Miss Barker.

"Good morning, Joan. How's your love life?"

"Oh!" exclaimed Miss Barker, and her fair skin went scarlet.

Conrad examined her more closely. She was slim and looked rather delicate. Her eyes bore evidence of the countless sleepless nights she had spent bent over her typewriter, working on his articles or on Gordon's memoranda. He had never noticed those dark circles under her eyes before. Perhaps they showed a little more clearly this morning as a result of the little airman's passion for her.

She was holding a paper parcel containing a couple of sandwiches and, thanks to her boy friend's generosity, a chocolate bar. These she would eat a little later, without leaving the office, as she drank the daily cup of tea the Editor of *Victory* charitably dispensed to every member of the staff. In the evening, work permitting, she would take off two hours to dine by herself in the canteen or in a local restaurant with her boy friend. After which, her bosses' requirements would keep her chained to her desk till the early hours of the morning. She never complained. She was proud of her personal contribution to a task she knew to be important, and working for a celebrated writer was such a fascinating job that she never admitted to feeling tired. Without knowing exactly why, Conrad was moved by her and decided to have a word with Gordon about cutting her working hours.

"Just a moment, Joan. I've got a few pages to be typed. But don't worry, I won't keep you long today."

"Thank you, sir," replied Miss Barker, as she went through to the office next door, where she performed her humble but by no means trivial duties.

Conrad sat wrapped in thought for a minute or two, then shrugged his shoulders and went on with his work.

The Royal Air Force provided him with a fresh subject for developing a number of arguments that his pen rendered all the more forceful. He quoted Churchill and described how, "at the most crucial moment in our history," when Britain formed the only bulwark against the onslaught of the powers of evil, a handful of heroes had won the battle of the skies, causing the enemy such losses that daylight raids were forthwith abandoned. Quality, in fact, had prevailed over quantity.

After dealing with the various European theaters of war, the fighting in the Western Desert, and the trouncing the Italians had been given, he could not very well leave out the recent events in the Far East. He was slightly disturbed to find that he could not in all honesty present these in an optimistic light. After debating the matter in his mind for some time, he decided not to wander off the beaten track. He did not minimize the gravity of the present situation, but instead stressed the value of the trump card Britain had just been dealt in the shape of the United States, whose entry into the war had been an immediate consequence of the Japanese attack. American intervention had not yet had time to produce any tangible results. That there were benefits to be derived from it in the very near future, however, he clearly demonstrated, with all the forcefulness he could muster. The decisive round would be fought out not in Singapore or Burma or Hong Kong but in Europe and Africa, both of which were direct lines of approach. To prove it, he described how several large convoys bound for Malaya had recently been diverted to reinforce the more important fronts. On these Britain's position was growing stronger every day. The Japanese empire would collapse automatically and immediately with the final defeat of Hitler.

He was about to embark on the conclusions to be drawn, to which he always paid particular care, when T. H. Gordon burst into the room in his usual whirlwind fashion and, without even saying good morning, announced that the hour had now come for Conrad to give his talents full rein.

Conrad's articles had caused a tremendous stir, so Gordon assured him as he drew up a chair, without bothering first to take off his hat.

"—and, what's more, in every section of the community, my lad," the Managing Editor jauntily declared.

"Every little shopgirl in London now swoons with delight every time your name's mentioned; all the lion-hunting hostesses think you're a wonder for expressing exactly what they themselves feel; and even their husbands have been won over by the force of your arguments."

Gordon looked upon this success as a personal triumph. He went on to say that the Propaganda Minister had been deeply impressed by the paper's ever-increasing influence and had at last decided to recruit a few worth-while assistants. God knows, he might have thought of that a little sooner—but, anyway, he had called for Gordon the evening before. He had started by congratulating him on the way he ran his paper, on the sound policy he had adopted, and on the high quality of the writing. This had only been a preamble to bring the conversation round to Conrad himself, who had once been fool enough to think of burying his talents among a lot of brass hats! The Minister had asked Gordon to convey his compliments to this illustrious colleague of his.

"This is what he said: 'Tell your friend Conrad that the Government is fully aware of his achievements and ability. Only this morning old Goodfellow was saying how surprised he and his wife were that this ability was not being put to better use. I absolutely agree with them. Unfortunately, I can't find a suitable place for him in the organization—' You realize what he meant by that, don't you?" Gordon interjected. "It's that damned foreign accent of yours; there'd be an outcry from the die-hard Tories.

" 'But if he's prepared to work for us in an unofficial capacity,' the Minister went on, 'we'd welcome his advice and be delighted to hear what suggestions he might have for reorganizing our internal and external propaganda. Later on, the Government will be in a position to recognize all services rendered in this field. Meanwhile, do ask him to work out a scheme and send it in to us.' Well, my boy, what do you say to that?"

At first Conrad could find no words to express what he wanted to say, so intense was the joy he felt at his success. To have the highest authorities, the actual leaders of an enemy nation, asking him to advise them on methods of psychological warfare! Not one of his chiefs could ever have hoped for such supreme success.

And since, in this perfectly balanced mind, initial instinct was quickly succeeded by rational thought, which in its turn led to practical planning, he was already working out a scheme to submit to the controllers of Britain's destiny. The task he had been allotted had not taken him unawares. Professionally interested in propaganda, he had for some time been studying the imperfections of the British system, its childishness and lack of punch. He had compared it with the achievements he had witnessed in his own country at the birth of the Party, with the clandestine activity he had organized in Danzig, and with his own personal experience in the course of his present mission. He already had in mind a number of reforms for which there was a crying need, which would give some semblance of life to the clumsy, halfhearted efforts whereby these dim-witted democrats were vaguely trying to demonstrate the justice of their cause. He devoted himself body and soul to this new assignment. He was genuinely appalled by the inefficiency he saw. He realized there was an urgent need for reorganization and could hardly wait to get down to work on it.

He told Gordon that he agreed and would start work that very evening. Alone again, he allowed himself no more than a fleeting moment of pleasure at this fresh confirmation of his ability before settling down to conclude his article, which he was anxious to get finished as soon as possible in order to have his mind free for other, more important matters.

His closing sentences reflected the enthusiasm he felt at what Gordon had just told him. Under the circumstances, how could one help feeling optimistic? The conclusion was self-evident. Even at this stage of the war, when the country's potential was not yet fully exploited, the enemy had been brought to a standstill and was being held in check. What, then, was the outcome likely to be when this potential could be exploited to the full?

In his summing up, which he tried to keep as restrained as possible, he drew attention to the following factors: the full-scale mobilization of the Anglo-Saxon world; the inexhaustible resources of the Dominions and colonies; the Empire's immense wealth in foodstuffs, raw materials, and oil; above all, the morale of the people, the superhuman effort that was being made at this very moment, not only by every member of the fighting forces, but by every civilian as well. In Britain, which Hitler had sneered at for its decadence and self-indulgence, there was not a single man over military age, not a single married woman or adult daughter, who was not devoting the greater part of his or her time and effort to the cause of liberty. That in itself would be enough to turn the scales. But, in addition, there was Russia, that vast and tireless Continental power, which was maintaining a stubborn resistance, and which, even on her own, would be more than a match for the Reich. And what of the immense potential represented by America? There was no need to dwell on the number of aircraft, ships, and tanks that her mighty industrial resources enabled her to build and throw into battle every month, every day, every minute of the day. With these trump cards in one's hand, it was virtually impossible to lose; and the first signs of victory were already quite apparent to anyone but a fool or a knave.

Conrad had written this last paragraph like a man inspired, with a facility that astonished him, and with such conviction that he began to feel almost unsure of his own loyalty. He stopped to think for a moment. A genuine patriot could not have put it over more forcefully, he concluded.

But this was no time for brooding. He dismissed the nagging doubt from his mind, read his article over again, and corrected it all the more conscientiously, remembering the Minister's message of congratulation. It was nearly two o'clock. He felt like having some lunch in the canteen downstairs, where he often ate at midday. He suddenly remembered how pathetic Miss Barker had looked, with the dark circles under her eyes and the packet of sandwiches in her hand, and decided to ask her to join him.

For form's sake he first approached Gordon, who said he did not need her for the time being. For a moment Conrad thought of taking her to a restaurant round the corner where the food would be a little better, but he felt the typist would be less concerned with good food than with the honor of being seen by the rest of the staff in his company. As they went into the dining room together, he realized from the sparkle in the girl's eyes that his assumption was correct. He occasionally showed this sort of consideration for others and had no particular objection to making people happy.

6

Sir Wallace was alone in his nondescript office. His half hour's nocturnal meditation had drawn out to three quarters of an hour, and finally an hour. He had not yet made a telephone call or drafted a single order. He could not decide on a definite line of conduct. Goodfellow can't make up his mind, he said to himself.

The office, with its cleanliness, tidiness, and carefully planned layout, could have served as a model for many commercial establishments. In the middle of the room there was a large table with a glass top—his desk. There were no drawers to the desk. Sir Wallace hated the very idea of drawers. In the middle of the table, in front of the chair, was a leather-bound writing pad, then a crescent-shaped blotter, a red pencil, a blue pencil, and a ruler. There was no inkwell, no penholder; he always used a fountain pen. On the left, within arm's reach, stood a square metal-wire tray marked "In"; on the right, symmetrically placed in relation to his swivel chair, a similar tray marked "Out." Whenever Sir Wallace got up to leave at the end of the day's work—which was any time between midnight and seven o'clock in the morning—both trays were empty, and there were no loose papers about.

To the left of his comfortably upholstered chair was a low table with two telephones on it. One of these was connected to the local exchange; the other was not. There was plenty of room for both of them on the desk, but Sir Wallace liked to spread himself when writing. On the other side of the desk, facing the window, was another armchair.

In one corner of the room, standing against the wall, was a steel cabinet with partitioned shelves. These pigeonholes contained a number of files, each carefully marked with certain algebraic signs that could be understood by two people only—Sir Wallace himself and his assistant, Mr. Jones, a conscientious young man of thirty. In the opposite corner, symmetrically placed in relation to the window—Sir Wallace had a passion for symmetry—stood a plain little desk with a typewriter. Mr. Jones often worked at this desk when his chief was away. But when he was there, as he was this evening, Mr. Jones' place was in the room next door, unless called for and asked for his advice on some point or other. For the most part Sir Wallace liked to work by himself, but occasionally he welcomed a second opinion.

A gray carpet, slightly worn but still quite serviceable, muffled the sound of footsteps. He hated any kind of noise. There was no other furniture in the room, except for a small safe standing against the wall on the left-hand side of the door. He hated clutter.

Sir Wallace was fifty-five years old. He liked everything to be clear-cut and straightforward—simple surroundings, clear thinking, and the direct speech that goes with it. Whenever he was called upon to disentangle some hopelessly involved situation, he was never satisfied until he had reduced every consideration to a small number of facts that could be logically linked together.

Mr. Jones himself was responsible for typing all the correspondence and reports, even though the office could easily have afforded a typist. But Sir Wallace refused to have women on his staff. In Mr. Jones he had complete confidence, a confidence based on certain facts that were not very widely known. He preferred to depend on him alone for the transmission of every order. It was Sir Wallace who gave the orders. The young man held the second key to the filing cabinet; on the other hand, Sir Wallace alone held the only key to the safe, which contained a certain number of top-secret documents.

A door in the wall on the right-hand side led into the other office. It was two o'clock in the morning. Mr. Jones was asleep in there on a camp bed. Sir Wallace had told him that he did not need him for the time being and had advised him to get a few hours' sleep. Mr. Jones was quite used to sleeping fully dressed. There was always someone on duty in the office at every hour of the night or day. On the rare occasions when Jones himself was away, his place was taken by J. Duncan.

J. Duncan was not there that night. Sir Wallace was never present when he was in. Duncan had never met him and did not know his name. Moreover, Duncan was not very good at paper work, and in his specialized field of activity he was often busy elsewhere.

Beside these two members of the staff, there were four middle-aged gentlemen—always the same four—who from time to time, but not very often, came in to hold a mysterious conference. On these occasions Mr. Jones moved the chairs out of his own room into the main office, then quietly disappeared. He was careful to put everything back in its place as soon as the last caller had left. He knew his chief could not bear the slightest sign of untidiness.

Sir Wallace was far from satisfied. In front of him was a red folder, sealed; on top of this a report, drafted and typed out by Mr. Jones. He read it over again for the third time:

"*G.Y.22 Weekly Report*

"*12 December.* Dined with Sir W. and Lady G. Others present were—" Inserted here was a list of the guests, followed by the note: "Nothing known against any of these or against the hosts, with whom he is on the closest terms.

"Left the party early to go to the *Victory* office. Saw Miss B., his secretary, on duty. Received two personal letters. Finished work and went home.

"*Remarks:* 1. Miss B. Nothing known against her. Girl friend of Flight-Lieutenant W., who gave Duncan the above information.

"2. The two letters. See copies, forwarded by Censor, in file together with Cipher Section's remarks. The first from Captain A. P. in Singapore, a regular correspondent. The other: sender unknown, trite compliments. No comments.

"*13 December.* Answered A. P.'s letter. See copy and remarks in file, with note as before.

"Long conversation with T. H. G., Managing Editor of the paper (Source: Miss B., quoted by her boy friend). Probably informed of the Minister's decision to make him unofficial adviser to propaganda reorganization.

"Lunch with Miss B. in office canteen. Unusual.

"*15 December*. With Lady G. went to a charity sale in aid of air-raid victims.

"*Other days:* Working in office. Seems extremely busy.

"*Conclusions:* Nothing new to report. Same contacts. Same show of loyalty. No *fact* to justify any suspicion. Still under surveillance."

Sir Wallace betrayed his irritation as he read these conclusions and muttered that only a fool would expect a show of disloyalty in these circumstances. He opened the folder and studied Cipher's notes on the letter Conrad had received a few days before:

"Sender does not give her address. Commonplace writing, women's magazine style. On the surface nothing suspicious. Particular points: a word scratched out, between brackets, which might or might not be a recognition signal—"

Sir Wallace for his part cursed these damned technicians for their own literary style.

"No possible conclusion at this stage. An isolated sample is not enough to show whether there is a concealed message or not. If possible, try and procure further letters same source."

Sir Wallace felt out of patience with these narrow scientific theories. On the spur of the moment he seized a sheet of paper and scribbled a few lines:

"Continue efforts to break code until further notice. Shall put an advertisement in *The Times* personal column asking unknown writer to send further letters."

After a moment's thought he scratched out the last sentence and methodically put the note into his "Out" tray.

He kept fingering the red folder, trying to make some sense out of all this rubbish, and was annoyed to find himself completely baffled. Telling himself to be patient, he went over all the documents from start to finish.

The first lot consisted of the official statements made by the Pole, William Conrad, on his arrival in England six years before. These were not of much interest. Sir Wallace went on until he came to a report from a certain European country that dealt with clandestine activity in Poland and mentioned the disappearance of a Nazi agent whose description tallied in many respects with Conrad's. This was one of the documents that had first roused Sir Wallace's interest. There was little to go on: no photograph and only a vague description. The agent who had furnished the information had meanwhile vanished into the blue himself, as a result of one of those accidents that occur from time to time in foreign parts. There was no hope of tracing the intelligence back to its original source; Sir Wallace had no illusions on that score. He was well aware that out of a hundred investigations initiated on such slender evidence no more than one ever led to anything; but that one was worth the unsuccessful ninety-nine. Besides, he could not help being struck by the coincidence. He always relied on his instinct, and his instinct told him there was something fishy about this business. Furthermore, in the safe to which he had the only key, there was another document from a different source, which no one was allowed to see, not even the devoted Mr. Jones. A certain passage in it seemed to confirm his suspicions—

only seemed to, for even on this point he could not be absolutely certain.

He had not been particularly impressed by Conrad's career and literary success or by the affection for his adopted country that was evident in everything he wrote. He had quickly gone through this period, which was represented in the folder by a series of short notes, and had come to the time when Conrad volunteered for the army. This had certainly taken him aback. He had wavered and almost given up. He knew that Mr. Jones would have given up if he had been in his position, and had been afraid he could already see an expression of amused contempt on his assistant's face. Nevertheless he had decided to carry on, and had made this decision known in such strong terms that further comment from Jones had been out of the question.

He now had before him a copy of Conrad's personal file from the O.C.T.U. at W———. It contained nothing but praise. He was not put in a better mood by reading yet again that this "brilliant young cadet has distinguished himself by his natural ability and keenness" or that "he is quick to understand every branch of military science and has outstanding qualities of leadership." For the umpteenth time he studied the note the Indian Army colonel had appended toward the end of the course: "He has shown a critical faculty and boldness of conception that in the whole of my long career I have never come across before in an officer of his age. Most junior officers are unable to master questions of higher strategy."

"Bloody old fool!" Sir Wallace muttered under his breath. He did not think much of Indian Army colonels. He went on reading: "This one, however, not only understands them but is capable of interpreting them as though he has always been familiar with them. Specially recommended for rapid promotion."

"Silly old ass!" Sir Wallace repeated, following a sequence of thought of his own. Yet in spite of his irritation, he carefully considered every word of this flattering report.

Friends and acquaintances. . . . One note was devoted to Arthur Patton's private life and public career—his academic activities, his professional colleagues. Not much in that. Conrad's behavior during the war—his active service; his citations; his wound and hospitalization; his meeting with Lady Goodfellow; a few details on their relationship. Sir Wallace shrugged his shoulders.

Conrad's appointment to *Victory*. A short note on the policy of this paper and the background of the managing editor. No further comment.

Patton's departure for the Far East. A thick packet was the last thing in the folder—the letters the two friends had exchanged. There was nothing in them to justify further comment, at least not from the professional point of view. But in the subjects discussed and the style of writing, Sir Wallace found plenty of room for criticism. He was particularly put out by Patton's digressions on natural science and the abstract arguments he used, which were abhorrent to his own realistic mind. Yet he felt it was his duty to try to make some sense out of all this idle chatter. Not that he really suspected Patton of anything—he, at least, was no doubt perfectly innocent, always assuming that there actually was a guilty person in this damnable affair—but he was G.Y.22's closest friend, after all. And you never could tell.

Sir Wallace went through the letters once more and heaved a sigh of despair at the sight of several sentences like the following: "When the Archaeopteryx had developed bird's feathers in place of its former membranes (and this, I assure you, was mainly achieved by will power), it thereby raised itself one degree higher in the animal hierarchy—"

Sir Wallace could scarcely control himself: "Archaeopteryx, indeed!" It was a painful reminder. He remembered the excitement this word had caused in the censorship department. The whole staff had been notified, and even he, Sir Wallace himself, had been forced to take the matter up, although he had very different fish to fry. But this suspect term had been followed by a number of foreign-looking proper nouns, such as Lamarck and Bauer. A little further on Hegel and Schopenhauer also cropped up; the censor's staff were not expected to be familiar with the names of these authorities. Sir Wallace, however, was sufficiently educated not to condemn Schopenhauer as a spy out of hand, and he knew something about Hegel's philosophy—necessary qualifications for the position he held. All the same, he could hardly be expected to know every single outlandish term in which these damned scientists referred to their discoveries!

He had never told a soul, however, that after being given a copy of that letter in the morning he had provided himself by the evening with a mass of material on the origin of species, evolution, and various other scientific theories. Cursing and swearing at the ridiculous position into which he been forced by his professional conscience, he had laboriously studied these difficult subjects, for he felt that only by tracing this jargon back to its source could he be certain that it did not contain some hidden meaning.

"Bloody fool!" he muttered once again, only this time he was referring to himself. That work had lost him several hours' sleep—he did not sleep much as it was—but he had never even considered assigning it to a subordinate.

He read Patton's last letter, found there was nothing of interest in it, closed the folder, and started thinking again. This evening he had devoted over two hours to G.Y.22. As a general rule, he did not personally deal with this kind of case. There were several departments under him that were perfectly capable of the task. But he had insisted on undertaking this one himself, since he felt that his subordinates were unlikely to show sufficient interest in it, because of the slender evidence at hand. Without knowing what the document in the safe contained, there was nothing but a personal impression to go on. Even with this document, the impression was anything but strong. Instinct was not considered a serious working basis in Sir Wallace's profession. He was chary of it himself, yet he was letting himself be guided by it now.

He felt like discussing the matter with someone else, but hesitated for a moment before waking Mr. Jones, whose hours of sleep were as limited as his own. He decided on a compromise. He called out without raising his voice, promising himself not to repeat the call if his assistant did not answer.

Mr. Jones was a light sleeper. Less than a minute later he appeared at the door, wide awake, neat and tidy, and apparently in the best of spirits.

"You called, sir?" asked Mr. Jones.

"Yes, Jones," Sir Wallace replied with a momentary

feeling of remorse. "I wanted to know what you think about all this. I've just had a look at your last report. There's not much in it. Did you see Duncan yourself? We're getting nowhere as far as I can see."

"Yes, sir, I saw him all right. We had a long talk. There's nothing else apart from what I've given you. Not the faintest hint of any suspicious activity. Nothing at all to suspect in G.Y.22's present behavior. But Duncan's still keeping a watch on all his contacts, according to your instructions, including Sir Wallace and Lady Goodfellow."

While he pronounced that last sentence, Mr. Jones did not allow his features to outline as much as the ghost of a smile. Sir Wallace looked at him for a moment and said with the same unconcern, "I hope he's being discreet about it, Jones?"

"You can count on Duncan, sir. He knows how you feel about security."

"Right, Jones. Now, what about the typist?"

"No fresh developments there, sir. Her life seems to be anything but mysterious. Our information on her comes from the source I mentioned in my report. She talks far too much about Conrad for us to suspect her of being a secret accomplice. And she's not the only one who thinks a lot of him."

"I know, Jones, I know. Lady Goodfellow also thinks very highly of him. He's a real lady-killer, this fellow. If I were to throw the slightest suspicion on his loyalty, if I were to venture ever so humbly the opinion that he was not perhaps all that he appears to be, do you know what would happen, Jones? I'd have my eyes torn out by a bevy of outraged harpies. I might even be relieved of my duties and asked to resign. Because he's an object of hero worship to certain men as well. There's a dear little don who has poured out his soul to him and sent him his love before going off into the jungle to be nibbled by the ants. And now the Government have given him an important assignment, just to prove their complete trust in him! I bet you're also taken in by him, Jones, you and Duncan as well; I bet you both think I'm a silly old woman who sees a spy around every corner and looks under the bed every night before going to sleep—when I do happen to sleep in bed, that is. Isn't that what you think, Jones?"

"Well, sir, you've no doubt got your own reasons and we know nothing about them, but you must admit that on the face of it—"

Sir Wallace interrupted him without raising his voice. In a special tone he used, which sounded all the more convincing, he said, "I'm convinced, I tell you, that there's something fishy about this business. You don't know the bloody Hun as I do, Jones. In this country we're inclined to consider people in terms of the average man; over there, each individual is treated as a special case. You never know what you're up against when you're dealing with foreigners. No grounds for suspicion, you say? Well, I've come across some men who've been able to hide their true feelings for years on end, Jones, who've managed to pass themselves off as rabid patriots, as loyal little boy scouts—until one day they slipped up somewhere. That's what I'm waiting for this fellow to do. And when he does, it's up to us to see that he doesn't get away with it. If I am mistaken, no one, apart from ourselves in this office, will ever know anything about it, and I don't give a damn what you or Duncan thinks about me. It was only to tell you this that I woke you up, Jones. We're going to press on with this case. And pass this on to Duncan as well. We've got to keep on our toes and be all the more on our guard. However innocent this fellow may seem, that's all the more reason for treating him as a suspect. Is that quite clear, Jones? I want the fullest information on him, even the most trivial details, day by day, hour by hour, minute by minute."

"Very good, sir. But if that's the case, shouldn't we warn the Propaganda Minister?"

"Not for the moment. Ministers aren't in the least interested in Intelligence. Their only concern is when we've got something definite to tell them, and so far there's nothing. All G.Y.22's propaganda suggestions will be reported back to us long before any action's taken on them. I've seen to that. I want to give him enough rope to hang himself. Perhaps this is where he'll come to grief. Well, good night, Jones; go back to sleep. Everything quite clear?"

"Quite clear, sir," said Mr. Jones, with a slight bow.

Sir Wallace got up. Before leaving, he made sure everything was in its place. He took the note he had drafted for the Cipher Section out of the "Out" tray and read it over again: "Continue efforts to break code until further notice."

The sentence was not entirely to his liking. He sat down again and added, "by every means at your disposal." After a moment's further thought, he took the red pencil and heavily underlined these last words.

"Here, Jones. Would you please type this and send it out early in the morning. Don't forget to underline in red, as I have done on the draft."

This done, he cast a final glance over his desk and at the safe, making sure that every paper was safely locked up and that the key was in his pocket.

"Good night, Jones," he said finally, and put on his hat.

"Good night, sir," replied Mr. Jones.

As soon as Sir Wallace was out of the office, Jones locked and bolted the front door, made sure all the windows were shut, and put out the light. Leaving the inner door ajar, he went back to his own room, stretched out on his camp bed, and went to sleep again.

7

New Year's Eve was one of those special occasions on which ladies and gentlemen broke the Lenten fast that had been ordained for the duration of the war. Christmas had been a rather sober affair, but on the last day of 1941, when the situation was as bad as it could be, the people of Britain decided to celebrate till dawn, just as though the situation were perfect.

The dinner Sir Wallace and Lady Goodfellow gave was almost like a prewar party. After secret consultation, the ladies had agreed to wear long dresses that had not seen the light of day for over a year and had certainly not been improved by this seclusion. Characteristically, the hostess was the only woman whose clothes were in faultless taste. Her plain black dress accentuated her tiny waist and made the others look positively frumpish beside her. Conrad paid her the most obvious compliment, which brought a sparkle to her eyes and a blush to her cheeks. The gentlemen did not go so far as to turn up in dinner jackets, but the baggy old suits they usually wore were abandoned for something more in keeping with the festive season.

Normal drink restrictions were lifted for the evening. In the drawing room before dinner, the Chairman of the National Recovery League himself set the example, and everyone did his best to reach a state of blissful euphoria, which in retrospect would help alleviate the hardship of yet another year of austerity. The whisky had been bought on the black market. Sir Wallace had done his guests proud, knowing that, this once, neither his friends nor his wife nor his conscience would disapprove, secretly hoping, too, that there would be enough left over from this overt orgy to keep his clandestine cupboard filled for some time to come.

They talked about the war—this was always the main topic of conversation—but only on its more amusing aspects, and everyone had a story to tell.

Colonel Field of the War Office described how, a few days before the Japanese landing in Hong Kong, there had been a sharp difference of opinion between the civilian authorities and the military commander. The latter had announced his intention of putting up a couple of concrete pillboxes at a particularly vulnerable point, which happened to be on the golf course. The local commissioner had hotly opposed such an act of vandalism, which would not only ruin the landscape but also spoil the British colony's favorite sport. A heated argument had ensued. After countless conferences, the problem had remained unsolved and was therefore referred to London. In the end the military commander had been forced to admit defeat, and the pillboxes had been built a little farther away, in a position of no strategic importance whatsoever but where they did not put the golfers off their game.

This story gave rise to a fair number of caustic comments on red tape in general and on the ridiculous sentimentality that blunted some of the best brains in the country. But it also caused a few sentimental smiles.

Sir Wallace then handed round cigarettes, seizing the occasion to bring up his favorite story, about cigarette tins.

At one time these used to be opened by means of a small triangular steel blade, which was fixed to the inside of the cover and worked by the pressure of one's thumbnail. Since the war this device had been modified, an unknown mastermind having had the inspiration to punch a small triangle out of the side of the cover itself, which did away with the blade and thumb pressure and considerably simplified the whole process. One had only to bend down this metal tongue with a nail file, or anything else that happened to be at hand, and then use it as a cutting blade. The savings due to this invention were simply unbelievable.

"Really?" said his guests, trying hard to show some interest in this fascinating piece of information. Sir Wallace forthwith launched into the manufacturing details, pointing out how many of these tin covers could be produced in an hour by one man working a simple machine. Colonel Field then provided a sample of his facetious critical faculty by maintaining that though the Treasury might possibly have benefited from this discovery to the tune of several thousand pounds, no one could tell how much time and patience were wasted every day in the clumsy attempts of wretched smokers to open their tins by means of this newfangled device. Sir Wallace denied the very idea. A heated discussion ensued, followed by a practical demonstration, which the old baronet carried out on a tin of Players Number Three. From his painful efforts and awkward handling, it appeared that there was something to be said for Colonel Field's contention. Sir Wallace himself admitted as much, which caused so much laughter that everyone had to have another drink to pull himself together.

The guests trooped into the dining room. Lady Goodfellow had arranged the table herself, with glittering crystal and gleaming silver as a reminder of prewar festivity. There was also a bunch of mistletoe hanging from the chandelier, a reassuring symbol of the good old days that brought a sentimental tear to every eye.

At a sign from their hostess, the guests quietly distributed themselves round the table. Then the ladies sat down, struggling to find room for their full skirts, while the gentlemen helped them, carefully sliding the chairs under their heavy frills and furbelows before sitting down themselves.

Each guest lifted his starched napkin to find on the plate underneath an appropriate little Christmas-stocking present, ingeniously chosen for them by their hosts. Colonel Field had a length of red ribbon, as a sign of his bureaucratic appointment; the naval officer, a small wooden propeller; Conrad, a schoolboy's pen. For Sir Wallace himself, his wife had prepared a special surprise. The Chairman of the National Recovery League exhibited, with a flourish, an old sardine tin, with its metal top still wound round its special opening key. There was a burst of applause, and Colonel Field had tears of laughter coursing down his cheeks for a good five minutes.

For once there was no shortage of anything. There was proper mint sauce with the roast lamb, and genuine French wine. There was unlimited butter. The pudding was a dream. The table was decorated with colored cracker bonbons, which were pulled as the port went round. Each bang produced yet another paper cap, which was put on with due solemnity.

The dinner went on until late at night. Everyone was eager to make the most of the evening, and when at last the company left the table, there was not much left in dish or bottle to put aside for National Recovery purposes, but every stomach and heart was full.

With a sense of well-being the guests went back to the drawing room, which was also decorated with a bunch of mistletoe. Sir Wallace only just had time to open the champagne and fill the glasses before midnight struck and the New Year was welcomed in. Forming a circle, with hands linked, the ladies and gentlemen sang "Auld Lang Syne" in a noisy, uninhibited chorus. They then sang it again more quietly, as though moved by the solemnity of the occasion. Colonel Field, who had been born in Aberdeen, sang it for them once more, this time in Highland dialect. Then each of the gentlemen kissed each lady in turn under the mistletoe.

To dispel the sentimental atmosphere created by this ritual, Lady Goodfellow suggested dancing. A record was put on the phonograph. The gentlemen chose their partners, and at that instant William Conrad realized he no longer hated the English.

The discovery came over him all of a sudden, with the abruptness and conviction of a revelation. He had sat down by himself in a corner of the room. He was not dancing—because of his bad leg, he said, but really because, as an idle spectator, he could yield more easily to the delicious drowsiness that had settled on him as a result of this homelike celebration. He felt drunk with happiness as he watched Lady Goodfellow gliding round the floor. It was no longer a conscious effort for him to live up to his assumed personality, and he suddenly found to his horror that he felt quite at home in these surroundings. Yet he could not bear the idea of being even an involuntary member of a society in which the gentlemen were all red-faced, levelheaded, dull-minded, and dim-witted, while all the ladies, with very few exceptions, looked exactly like the gentlemen. He made a determined effort to master his feelings. He overcame the trouble that was pervading his German soul and managed to pull himself together. After thinking it over, he realized that he could not have immersed himself more completely in the part that he had to play. This was only what his masters had advised him to do. The important thing was to be able to recover consciousness at a moment's notice if necessary.

The party broke up as it was getting light. After giving an exhibition of the Highland fling, Colonel Field declared he had had a marvelous time. Then, claiming the privilege of age, he once again gave every lady in the room a kiss. Finally, he took off his paper cap and resumed the dignified expression he normally wore to keep junior officers in their place. He solemnly wished everyone a happy New Year and marched out into the dawn with a brisk stride that only just betrayed the amount of whisky he had consumed. He had confided he had to attend an important conference that morning and only had time for a quick shave, a bath, and a change of clothes. This was the sign for everyone to leave, and Conrad set out in the direction of his flat, trying hard to keep his thoughts at bay.

8

"*3 January.* Received another letter from Captain A. P. See copy from Censor. No fresh developments."

Sir Wallace was appalled to see how long the letter was. Five, six, seven pages! Prying into other people's correspondence was a job he hated; yet he had to do it, if only to get some idea of the writer's mentality. With a sigh of resignation he embarked on Patton's latest letter:

"My dear William,

"That native rag-and-bones merchant was right, and our local politicians were wrong. Here we are, retreating before the Mikado's little warriors. In fact, we're at war, just like you vulgar people in Europe. I've snatched a moment to write to you, since I don't know when I'll have a chance to write again. I'm very well and am actually enjoying seeing something of the interior of the country at last, though hardly under ideal circumstances. My only worry is that I've had to

leave my books behind; they're too unwieldy for jungle warfare. Well, I'll just have to do without them.

"As a matter of fact, I'd already given up reading, because it seems to me that no book, however good, is as valuable as personal experience. Let me try to put it more clearly. You can read and reread the same statement hundreds of times without attaching any importance to it. All you get from seeing it in print is a mental picture of certain facts, but you don't give a thought to the universal law, the basic idea, of which those facts are only the material consequences. On the other hand, if you are made aware of it through some sort of personal contact, it's like an overwhelming revelation, a regular feast for further thought.

"I hope you realize this preamble is only an excuse for telling you about my own personal experience. It's like this. In the last few weeks before I left Singapore, I went out quite a lot to the various clubs there. I made friends with some of the local residents and the planters who come in from time to time when they've had enough of living all alone upcountry. Well, this is what I've discovered: There's nothing I can tell you about these people—the officials, businessmen, etc.—that you don't already know yourself. Absolutely nothing. They're exactly the same as the chaps we used to meet in camp or on leave in London. They're not the slightest bit changed by being transplanted out here, which is so completely different from home. They're utterly impervious to local environment, and even after several years haven't

acquired a single Oriental habit or vice. The Singapore banks are like the banks in the City. The shops are like the shops in London. The clubs are like any English club, except for the fans. The members even dress like Englishmen, though their clothes are a little bit lighter than they would be at home. Everyone wears a tie, and I'm told that even in the most remote plantations people change for dinner every evening. From all this I draw the obvious conclusion that we English are insensible to any surroundings apart from our own.

"That's just the sort of truism you come across in books without giving it a second thought. Any foreigner could have told you that ages ago, you'll probably say. But even though I'd already been told it time and time again, I'd never really apprehended it. I have now; and as you know what I'm like, you won't be surprised to hear that I've been trying hard to determine the real idea, the philosophical significance, of this singular phenomenon.

"I'm not sure what to make of it yet. Perhaps you could help, since your own career happens to be a case in point. I know you won't take offense when I say that in spite of being born and brought up as a foreigner you're now far more English than the English themselves. The environment has caught hold of and remolded you completely. You've adopted our customs, our language, even our way of thinking. The opposite hardly ever happens. Why is this? The French, the Poles, the Russians, and even the Germans are individually just as cultured and intelligent as we are. Then what's the reason?

"Let me tell you what I think it is. I believe that only in the phenomenon of evolution, the phenomenon that transcends every other natural manifestation, can the answer be found."

"Here we go again!" grumbled Sir Wallace. "This chap can't write more than a dozen coherent sentences without going off at a tangent about transcendency or something. Still, for a philosopher, he didn't start off too badly."

"I think we belong to one of those rare subdivisions of humanity that has reached such a state of biological cohesion that it's ready to move from the individual plane to the higher, collective level. Most nations haven't developed much beyond the individual state. They're rather like separate protozoic cells that have conglomerated to a certain extent, I grant you, but that are still not united, still not fused into a single, collective body. They haven't yet managed to contribute naturally and involuntarily to the creation of a collective life force, in spite of their leaders' efforts to set such a force in motion by artificial means. We English are beginning to recognize ourselves as elements of a multicellular organism. The rough conglomeration has been molded together, rounded off, and reshaped so as to form the beginnings of a homogeneous whole. With the passage of time the various separate cells have settled down quite comfortably, each in its natural place, held together by the bonds they have in common. That explains why we're hardly ever affected by those violent conflicts between the individual and society, which in other countries are the main cause of quite a lot of private suffering and

most public disaster. Our nation has got over the difficult teething stage and so can afford to smile at the tantrums this childish complaint provokes in others.

"Now that the Russians and even the Old Goat himself have realized this aspect of evolution (which to me has always been self-evident), they're trying to bring the organism to life by scientific theory and brute force. Which proves I'm not so stupid, after all, for you can see for yourself that consciously or unconsciously this sort of effort is one of the main preoccupations of our era. But are they any nearer this regeneration than we are? Is it, in fact, possible to accelerate a gradual process by systematically directed action? Personally, I think it is possible, but it needs a vast amount of experience; without it, such action might be harmful—in this case it would be fatal—because of its lack of universal applicability.

"Samuel Butler, you remember—"

"Another of these bloody philosophers!" growled Sir Wallace.

"—maintains that heredity, both moral and physical, is only a form of memory. The reasons he gives are quite plausible, and I'm pretty certain his theory is valid, even though it leads to some pretty odd conclusions. If what he says is true, then the development of the human eye is due to the embryo's recollection of the efforts his earliest forefathers made to achieve the gift of sight when they themselves were still devoid of that particular organ. You've only got to transfer this theory from the individual plane and apply it to group level to realize that in us, too, there's a whole

mass of memories exactly like those leading up to the emergence of man, only on a larger, community scale. We've had our invaders, our conquerors, ages ago. We've had our wars and revolutions, our dictatorships and constitutional governments. We've dethroned our kings and we've also restored them. For countless years and in countless ways we've been striving toward a goal of which we were not even dimly conscious but that would eventually emerge as distinctly as the gift of sight in individual man. We've built one empire, and then destroyed it. This is our second. As a nation, we're said to be past our prime. But everything is relative, and old age may simply be another term for the attainment of maturity.

"Other races also have their recollections, but they don't seem to be as numerous or as varied as ours, and they're certainly not so collective. I don't believe their national memory is strong enough for them to be able to evolve an eye, still less a brain, and, least of all, the multicellular organism that in our case, I'm sure, is already in an advanced state of development. Who knows? it may even be nearing completion. Anyway, its effects can be felt already.

"Perhaps it's because we're an island race that we've been able to accelerate the process of gestation and facilitate the birth of this organism. Perhaps it's because the size and shape of our country provide us with a concrete symbol, and our spiritual unity is the inevitable outcome of this symbolic physical unity."

"What the hell is he getting at now?" moaned Sir Wallace.

"Whatever the reason, I'm convinced that the char-

acter of our country is not simply the sum total of the characters of its individual inhabitants. It's a combination, not merely a heterogeneous mixture—an abstraction, if you like, but an abstraction that proceeds from power. I shouldn't be at all surprised, I assure you, if it eventually developed into a material organism and finally gave birth to what we call true existence. I don't think this can happen overnight; but don't forget that behind us we've got only five hundred million years at the most, while there are at least ten thousand millions to look forward to in the future. In that space of time it would be absurd not to expect even stranger developments than the evolution of man from a mass of amoeba.

"I seem to have wandered a little off my original subject—our fellow countrymen in Singapore—but only a very little. The imperceptible cohesive quality of our environment explains why it has so much power not only over ourselves, by protecting us against outside influences, but also over foreigners, who involuntarily surrender themselves to it. That's why the English out here drink whisky but don't smoke opium. That's why you, old boy, and several others like you, write masterpieces in the English language.

"It's probably also the reason why our government officials denied the possibility of a Japanese invasion right up to the last moment, and why they're generally so incompetent and completely out of touch with local affairs. Well, I think that's enough for today. I hope to have further news for you in my next letter. We're moving off again now.

"I very nearly forgot to mention the Japanese. They're an island race like ourselves. Do you think they've contributed to the creation of a life force? I wonder!

"Yours ever,

"Arthur Patton

"P.S. *A definite sign that the process of fusion has already started is the fact that all our great scientists are poets—Jeans and Dunne, for instance—and all our poets are philosophers. What is a philosopher? I wish I knew!"*

Sir Wallace put the letter down on his desk and tried to imagine how a Nazi agent would react after reading it. He shrugged his shoulders. "Stuff and nonsense!" He read the last few paragraphs over again, and a twinkle came into his eye. "All the same, this fellow knows what he's talking about when he starts on government officials. If only he'd stick to that!"

9 Conrad embarked on his scheme for the reorganization of the propaganda department with the same zest and attention to detail that he devoted to every other undertaking. He enjoyed this sort of creative work and felt a strange, rather perverse, pleasure in being able to perform such a feat of dissimulation. The first draft was already done. He planned to submit it the following day at a top-secret conference to be attended by a number of V.I.P.'s. That evening he put the finishing touches to it in his office in the *Victory* building, while Miss Barker rattled away on her typewriter in the room next door.

As usual, he had done much more than had been demanded of him. He had not confined himself to making suggestions and giving advice but had mapped out a complete working program, divided into two main parts, the first dealing with internal propaganda, the second with external.

For the internal, he had advocated the official recruitment of every available specialist who was in touch with the general public or capable of dictating popular opinion. In a short introduction he demonstrated the need for giving a definite direction and positive slant to every policy, instead of leaving it, as it had been left till then, to individual initiative. In the intellectual field, which included propaganda, unity of purpose was as indispensable as unity of command on the field of battle. The ideology of the Germans should be countered by a doctrine based on the inviolability of human life and individual liberty. This ideal should be stressed in all its different aspects and instilled into every man, woman, and child in the country.

After this introduction Conrad dealt one by one with the various available means of achieving this end: newspapers, public lectures, political speeches, broadcast talks, educational films. For each of these methods of mass dissemination he envisaged a team of specialists directed by a central board of control that would be responsible for overall co-ordination. The articles, the talks, the broadcasts, and the films would form essential parts of a single composite whole in which each element would stress its own particular aspect of the British ideal. As an example, he suggested a number of articles for publication in various journals of different political views, and showed how these could be inserted by degrees so as to give the effect of a gradual build-up. He outlined suitable subjects for a series of documentary films and broadcast talks, which were to be given by political figures as well as by military leaders, so as to appeal to the civilian population as much as to the armed forces. Each of these would contribute its quota of moral mass persuasion. All this would have to be prepared in advance and in such a way as to make each isolated fact appear as the confirmation of an unswerving and unshakable unity that was bound to result in victory. The inference to be drawn was that victory depended on the excellence of the cause, and this should be put across to the people as a foregone conclusion. The result would be an immediate intensification of effort.

The external-propaganda system also needed to be thoroughly overhauled and recentralized. A special unit was required for selecting, maintaining, and co-ordinating the available intellectual equipment and for distributing it at regular intervals to the country's representatives overseas. Conrad outlined the sort of directives that should be sent to these representatives. He gave a rough indication of the direction and form British action should take in the neutral countries, where public opinion was of paramount importance, not only because it could be aired quite openly but also because those countries represented an unknown potential that could actively influence the course of the war. Hitler had already catered to this by employing some of his most competent specialists to direct propaganda in these countries. Finally, in the countries with which Britain was at war or which were hostile to her, Conrad proposed establishing a network of special agents, independent of the intelligence service, with whom they were not to be confused, but still subject to the central board of control. These would be responsible for disseminating documentary and other material specially designed to persuade the masses of the enemy's moral and physical superiority.

When it came to drafting this last section, Conrad had

his own personal experience to draw on. Here again he was not content to give only a rough outline but went into every detail, using actual examples to show how judicious exploitation of incidental factors could lead to important results.

All in all, it was quite a considerable work, original in conception but based on established authorities. Conrad read it over again, applying his highest standards of criticism to see whether it could be improved in any way, and concluded with a certain amount of self-satisfaction that nothing approaching this had ever been produced in England before.

He could not very well work the scheme out in further detail until he knew for certain that the Government approved of it. His immediate aim was to convince them, the leaders of the country first of all, that his suggestions were worth while. He could see nothing wrong with them himself. He had put into them the best that his brain, experience, and talent could provide. His only concern was whether they were set forth sufficiently clearly and cogently to force a unanimous decision in their favor. He knew what it was like at these high-level conferences, where every item was minutely examined, debated, and weighed in the balance by an impartial, objective, and open-minded body of men who were ready to consider any new or attractive idea that they had not thought of themselves. He believed his draft would appeal to them.

On second thought, however, he felt it was a little too dry, a little too technical, and that the V.I.P.'s who had asked him for these suggestions would probably be expecting something rather more vivid and original.

After all, he was a professional writer with a reputation for imaginative brilliance, and politicians would be the last people to mind if he did not adhere absolutely slavishly to technical matters. A note of fancifulness would probably not be amiss, and they would also no doubt welcome a digression or two outside the scope of routine business if he could introduce these with sufficient skill and enhance their emotional appeal by giving them a psychological twist. He had not forgotten the spiritual element when drafting his scheme; in fact, he had presented it as the fundamental basis of all propaganda. But he felt he had not emphasized the point sufficiently.

He felt it to be a sufficiently popular subject to justify a whole section to itself. He was well aware that many of these forthright, dispassionate men were fascinated when confronted with the brilliancy of abstract ideas. And, besides, to his own way of thinking, this spiritual factor was of fundamental importance. He was eagerly longing to lay stress on it, realizing that without it his work would have been reprehensibly incomplete. A passion was compelling his talent to reach a sort of sublime in duplicity, to blaspheme his own gods, glorify a false and beggarly ideal, and give a semblance of light and truth to the shoddy and contemptible cause for which these poor blind fools were fighting.

He finally decided to write a short preface, in which to summarize and stress the essential purposes of propaganda as he saw them. Without further ado he got down to work.

Lawrence of Arabia provided him with an appropriately unexpected opening that he felt was not unworthy of his subject. A few days before, he had come across a passage in *The Seven Pillars of Wisdom* and had been prompted by his professional conscience to make a note of it. He now quoted it as an example of the importance men of action attached to psychological persuasion:

"Some of it [our propaganda] concerned the crowd, an adjustment of its spirit to the point where it became useful to exploit in action, and the predirection of this changing spirit to a certain end. Some of it concerned the individual, and then it became a rare act of human kindness, transcending, by purposed emotion, the gradual logical sequence of the mind. It was more subtle than tactics, and better worth doing, because it dealt with uncontrollables. . . . We had to arrange their minds in order of battle just as carefully and as formally as other officers would arrange their bodies. . . . We must also arrange the minds of the enemy, so far as we could reach them; then those other minds of the nation supporting us behind the firing line, since more than half the battle passed there in the back; then the minds of the enemy nation waiting the verdict; and of the neutrals looking on; circle beyond circle."

Conrad felt this passage was admirably suited to his purpose. The opinion of a national hero was almost bound to impress the committee and, in view of the man's romantic, almost legendary character, also whet their appetite for what was to follow. In his anxiety to take them by surprise with a startling introduction, Conrad had even weighed the possibility of drawing on his master, Adolf Hitler, for a few carefully chosen words on methods of mass indoctrination; the value of his theories had been proved, and there was nothing to prevent their being put to good use in time of war. On second thought, however, Conrad had preferred to rely on Lawrence. With their genuinely objective outlook, these gentlemen were always prepared to recognize any good point in enemy procedure, but *Mein Kampf* was bound to carry less weight with them than *The Seven Pillars of Wisdom*. Besides, the idea Conrad was trying to put across was expressed almost as succinctly in this short excerpt as in the *Führer's* formal declarations. After drafting a brief comment on it, Conrad went on to his main, all-absorbing subject.

"In this particular conflict the enemy is following a specific doctrine, the racial doctrine: a definite ideal, a belief in the ultrahuman destiny of the German nation. Although this is a self-centered and morally invalid doctrine, it gives the German masses a sense of national unity that their leaders are forever extolling and that largely contributed to their initial success."

Conrad stopped for a moment to consider the telling power of each of these words, then went on:

"But what is the situation in this country, gentlemen? The honor I feel at being invited to give an opinion will not allow me to pass over in silence what I consider to be one of our weakest points. We, too, have a doctrine to follow. We, too, have our ideals, which have nothing in common with the arbitrary Nazi beliefs. Our ideal is faith in the high destiny of all humanity and not merely of one particular section of it. Our doctrine is recognition of human values and respect for individual freedom, without which our ideal could never be achieved. We are all aware of this, gentlemen, I know, and we feel these values are the only true ones, because they are universal. But perhaps it is just because we are so convinced of their truth that we feel it is superfluous to propagate them among the masses or to draw attention to the countless different aspects of them that happen to be obvious to us. That is a very grave mistake on our part, gentlemen. That is where we are seriously at fault. By our silence, or by the lack of feeling in our non-committal public statements, we are failing to maintain that sense of national unity that is the mainspring of all morale."

He went into this theme in greater detail, drawing on his wide knowledge of mass psychology. It could be argued that appreciation of these values was a natural instinct in free and civilized people. Quite so. That, precisely, was the fundamental difference between the ready-made pseudophilosophy of National Socialism and the natural, essentially human outlook of the free world. But a feeling that was never expressed became vague and unimportant. A true idea that no one would put into words was less likely to be believed than a constantly repeated lie. The enemy's success in Europe was a case in point; it was mainly due to the devilish cunning of his propaganda. His initial victories were a typical example of the triumph of an idea, no matter what that idea happened to be; the Rhineland, Austria, Czechoslovakia, and finally France, had all been infected by it.

At this stage in his argument certain phrases of Patton's unaccountably flashed through Conrad's mind, and in this way some of his friend's judgments unwittingly crept into his own writing:

"Hitler even believed he could contaminate this nation with his doctrine and thereby bring us to our knees. Certain statements of his reported by Rauschning leave no room for doubt on that score. But it is here, gentlemen, that Hitler made his big mistake. There is something about this country, some intangible element in its people, that instinctively reacts against outside influences. Of its own accord, and without demanding any effort on our part, our environment forms a protective barrier round us. This stability is possibly due to our being in a more advanced state of evolutionary development than other nations.

"All the more reason, then, to strengthen this natural advantage by drawing attention to it and making every individual British subject deeply aware of it. If the propagation of a lie has results, how much more can be expected from the skillful dissemination of the eternal truths for which we are fighting!

"Our doctrine and our ideal," Conrad concluded, "are both quite clear. They only demand to be stated. There is no need to express them in a different form; we only have to stress the truth. This is a perfectly straightforward task and requires only a little deliberation and psychological insight. It would be criminally negligent not to make use of such a weapon in the interests of victory. Stressing an ideal is to my mind the sacred aim of all propaganda, and it is with this conviction that I submit the following scheme."

If Conrad had listened to the voice of his inspiration, he would have developed this theme still further. Reason, however, told him that he had pursued it far enough to rouse interest and provide food for thought. The typescript to be distributed to the members of the committee would therefore end at this point, but he planned to make a number of additional verbal comments during the general discussion at the end of the meeting.

He went over the text of his address, conscientiously

reading it out loud to himself. He could find no fault with it and was particularly pleased with the note of conviction his message carried. But this pleasure was accompanied by an odd, rather unpleasant sensation: a vague feeling of remorse, a dull ache at the bottom of his German heart, which seemed to be holding this note of conviction against him.

This put him in mind of the Fatherland. When would his lords and masters finally decide to contact him? After all, he had now prepared the ground. This ridiculous situation could not go on forever. There were moments when he could hardly bear the discomfort of his split personality.

He tried to dismiss these thoughts, which could do nothing but harm his mission. "After all," he concluded, "there's no hurry. The longer I wait, the stronger my position will be."

Pulling himself together, he realized it was close on midnight.

"Joan!" he called out.

"Yes, sir?" Miss Barker came in from the room next door. He assumed an earnest, almost paternal, expression.

"Joan, I'm terribly sorry about giving you this to type at such an unearthly hour, but it has taken me longer than I thought, and I simply must have it back by tomorrow afternoon, or even earlier if there are any corrections. I believe Mr. Gordon spoke to you about it, didn't he?"

"Yes, sir. He told me to give it top priority and drop anything else I was working on."

"Here it is then, Joan. Careful about the punctuation, as usual. I don't know whether Mr. Gordon told you, but it's rather important and strictly confidential. I'm giving it to you to do because I know you and I know I can trust you. But I ought to tell you, Joan, that rather than give it to anyone else I should have typed it out myself. So treat it as top secret, please, and keep it to yourself. Is that quite clear, Joan?"

"Quite clear, sir."

She counted the sheets and made a rapid mental calculation.

"If you like, sir, I could get this done tonight. It shouldn't take more than three or four hours."

"I didn't dare ask you myself, Joan. But if you're not too tired, it would be better. Bring your machine in here, then I'll be able to correct it as we go along. That'll save us a little time."

"Thank you, sir," said Miss Barker.

She came back with her typewriter and sat down opposite him, completely dazed by this unexpected privilege. Helping in a really important top-secret job and working hand in glove with her hero! She even forgot to ring up her boy friend to tell him she would be on duty and therefore could not meet him that evening.

The young airman was waiting for her, trying to think what to ask her without rousing her suspicions, so as to have something to satisfy Duncan's curiosity. He had been working for Duncan ever since being grounded as a result of his wound. His new job was sometimes wonderfully exciting, but he hated his present assignment. He consoled himself with the thought that there was a war on and that Joan was really quite good fun. He had not been let into the secret completely; Duncan had simply told him that William Conrad was the target of some deep-laid plot the service was trying to unearth and that for this purpose detailed information was required. The flight-lieutenant did his best to provide it without bothering too much about the reason.

As his girl friend had still not turned up, he whiled away the time by dipping into the bag of candy he had brought for her. When it was finished, he went to sleep so quickly that he did not have a chance to feel cross with her.

10

J. R. Beckett was at work in his room.

J. R. Beckett did not have an office and had no fixed working hours. He was part of the Cipher Section, yet remained his own master. J. R. Beckett was one of those "available means" Sir Wallace had referred to in his note to the section. When he underlined those words in red—which was not a usual habit of his—he was thinking of J. R. Beckett. He had never met him—he had no need to—but he knew him well by reputation.

J. R. Beckett's personal contribution to the war effort was his gift of second sight; his enemy was the concealed message. The Cipher Section boasted quite a number of specialists with second sight, each of whom had to his credit a long list of exploits that were unknown to the general public though nonetheless of far-reaching consequence. There was hardly a document in existence from which they were unable to extract the spirit that might be concealed in its apparently innocuous wording. Their ability was the result of long experience, familiarity with a multitude of coding systems, patience in juggling countless cipher groups, close attention to messages with a common peculiarity, common or garden intuition, and many other factors besides.

But occasionally they were forced to admit defeat. Their powers deserted them, the code refused to be broken. It was at times like this, if the matter was sufficiently important, that the head of the section had recourse to certain back-room boys, who were held in reserve for any outstanding case. There were not very many of them; at this time there were not more than three in the whole of London. J. R. Beckett was one of the three, and the most highly valued.

J. R. Beckett was a man of medium height and medium build, with a head that in no way suggested it contained a brain of abnormally large capacity. He ate the same as anybody, slept the same as anybody, drank beer and whisky the same as anybody. He did not drink a great deal of coffee. He did not take drugs. He did not smoke opium, only an occasional pipe of tobacco. He was not very fond of music. He was moderately good at chess. He had once been fairly interested in mathematics but had given it up after being told at school that he had not a hope of succeeding in this subject because of his weakness in logic: He could often see the solution of a problem quite clearly—a solution that seemed absolutely obvious—but he was incapable of showing how he had arrived at the answer or demonstrating step by step his sequence of thought from hypothesis to conclusion.

At one time J. R. Beckett had been a humble civil servant who fulfilled his functions perfectly efficiently but was not particularly remarkable in any other respect.

Now he occupied a senior position on the Cipher staff and possessed a reputation that was too well-established to be undeserved. Sir Wallace himself, who considered discipline and punctuality of paramount importance even for those employed on special duties, had issued standing orders that J. R. Beckett was to be allowed to work in his own time, that he was to be promptly and without further question provided with any information he required, that he was to be given an adequate salary to relieve him of all financial anxiety. Those were the Director's orders. For him to have issued such a decree, there must have been some good reason; and indeed the few people who knew how much J. R. Beckett was really worth did not find these orders at all out of place.

When a message refused to deliver its secret even to the best technicians on the staff, it was sent to J. R. Beckett and then forgotten until he chose to announce the result of his investigations. It was delivered to him by hand—he hardly ever bestirred himself—together with a file containing the findings of the specialists who had worked on it and been defeated, the particular problems and dilemmas with which they had been faced, and the possible reasons for their lack of success. The message and file was returned after an unspecified length of time, either a few hours or else several weeks, together with J. R. Beckett's conclusions. These conclusions could be either positive or negative. The number of times they had turned out positive fully justified the reputation he enjoyed.

J. R. Beckett was at work in his room.

His room was at the same time his office and reference library. Since joining the Cipher Section he had been prompted by his professional conscience to examine the various methods used by his colleagues. Even though his initial successes were due almost exclusively to his own native intelligence, he had felt it was necessary to supplement this with the knowledge and experience of others. He had mastered all the processes known to the solvers of this particular kind of puzzle. He had learned several foreign languages. He did not speak them fluently but was sufficiently familiar with each to be able to find his way about the intricacies of syntax and vocabulary. With countless dictionaries and grammars within arm's reach there was no need for him to go into the subject more deeply. He had also made a study of the classic coding systems; and here again he had not attempted to learn every detail by heart. He had simply taken notes. All he wanted to know about them was summed up in the exercise books he had filled in longhand. He occasionally had recourse to these references; these tools of the trade were sometimes fairly useful, but hardly ever useful enough. His best results had been achieved because of some innate quality that owed nothing to learning.

This quality was an imponderable that was difficult to define; he himself could not quite explain it. It was too complicated simply to be dismissed as a natural gift. It certainly owed something to what his mathematics master had scornfully referred to as intuition. It included a dash of imagination, too—not the romantic sort of imagination that builds castles in the air, but an imagination capable of blazing a trail in the direction of fact instead of fancy. Were this quality to be carefully dissected, it would be found to contain something else besides: a deep psychological insight. Was it a sixth sense or the fruits of experience that enabled him to understand, to realize, to determine, to divine, to see—at any rate, to know, *a priori* and often with complete accuracy, the way in which a particular brain must have reacted in a given set of circumstances and the consequences that must have resulted, in the form of the particular choice of words that were the clue to every puzzle?

J. R. Beckett was at work in his room.

For the moment his work consisted of pacing up and down from one wall to another. He had decided not to go out at all that day and had put on a dressing gown. There was nothing very special about this garment apart from its shabbiness. He was smoking a Woodbine. On his table was a photostatic copy of the fan letter Conrad had received a few days before. The covering file, marked "Strictly Confidential," did not give him much information. It simply outlined the recipient's personal particulars and stated there was no known connection between him and the sender—which was one of the main reasons for Sir Wallace's passionate interest in it. There was also a summary of the tests that had been made, so far without result. A final note gave him to understand that although the "responsible authority" was determined to pursue the investigation by every possible means, it was quite possibly a wild-goose chase and the message might be perfectly innocuous.

J. R. Beckett felt rather annoyed as he read this last sentence. He had no objection to sweating over a text for a fortnight with only a few hours' sleep, but he did like to know where he stood. Delving into a mystery sharpened his wits. But the prospect that there might not even be a mystery acted on him like a cold shower, damping his enthusiasm for getting at the truth. He cursed the senior officer who had drafted that note. A technician ought to know better. He promised himself that if he ever had to issue an instruction himself, he would try to be a little less discouraging. He thought of the "responsible authority" and wondered whether he would have sanctioned this wording.

J. R. Beckett had not managed to shake off his lethargy when there was a ring at the door of his flat—if the combination of a bedroom, a bathroom, and a minute kitchen, which also served as an entrance hall, could be described as a flat. He carefully put the papers away in a drawer, locked them up, put the key in his pocket, and went to open the door. He had no servant. He had to go through the kitchen himself to let his visitor in. It was Mr. Jones.

J. R. Beckett had already met Mr. Jones—since Sir Wallace had to remain in the background, his assistant inevitably dealt with outside contacts. J. R. Beckett remembered Mr. Jones' face. He was not quite sure of his functions; they were no concern of his. But he did know that he held quite an important subordinate position and that he had the ear of the "responsible authority." He showed him into the room without further ceremony.

Mr. Jones came quickly to the point. He explained the purpose of his visit in a nutshell, with a note of authority in his voice that was justified by his privileged position, but also with the deference due to a man of J. R. Beckett's reputation.

"I've come about this G.Y.22 business. I believe Cipher sent you the file this morning?"

It was part of Mr. Jones' duties to keep himself informed of every internal communication directly or indirectly connected with Sir Wallace. He could not go into them all in detail, but the interest his chief showed in the case of G.Y.22 had prompted him to follow it up step by step.

J. R. Beckett acknowledged receipt of the documents, and Mr. Jones went on, "The Director doesn't think the covering note was sufficiently explicit."

J. R. Beckett pricked up his ears. He was beginning to feel a little more interested.

"The Director thinks this case is extremely important, so important in fact that he has taken the unusual course of going over the head of the Cipher Section and sending me here to give you his personal instructions by word of mouth."

Mr. Jones tried to remember Sir Wallace's exact words and found himself unconsciously copying the Director's persuasive manner.

" 'Tell him,' the Director said, 'that this letter *has* got a double meaning and that it *does* contain a concealed message. It's up to the experts to decipher it. I'm absolutely certain of this, and I've got every reason to be—but that's my own business.' That's what he told me to tell you. He was afraid Cipher weren't quite convinced of the nature of the letter."

"They certainly aren't. Their comments seem to suggest that the letter's probably harmless. Tell the Director I quite understand and that I'll do my very best."

J. R. Beckett was lost in admiration for this perspicacity, this psychological insight, on the part of the "responsible authority." Mr. Jones also profited by his example and made a mental note to model his own conduct on his if ever he should become a director himself.

Meanwhile, there were a few additional details that Sir Wallace had asked him to explain in order to give as complete a picture as possible. He explained them and then left, after wishing the other good luck.

A few minutes later J. R. Beckett was interrupted in his work by a second ring. This time it was the telephone. An unknown voice asked him, "Is that you, Beckett? Has Jones been to see you yet?"

Cautiously, J. R. Beckett refused to answer. The voice persisted in a more commanding tone:

"It's the Director speaking. I want to know whether you've understood what Jones had to tell you. I want to hear you in person say that there's now no doubt in your mind, no matter what you were told before, about the subject we're both interested in. Is that clear, Beckett?"

J. R. Beckett smiled to himself as he answered. "It's all quite clear, sir. I take it you're anxious to have a positive result?"

The voice dropped its commanding tone and became almost pleading. "That's it, Beckett; that's it. A positive result. The fact is, I can't tell you how important this business is. I *know* it's rather a problem, but I *must* have it solved. You realize what I'm driving at, Beckett?"

The expert assured him he would do his best.

"That's it, Beckett. Do your best, more than your best, even. You know what that means as well as I do. It'll be worth while, I promise. Well good-by, Beckett, and good luck."

This telephone call gave some indication of Sir Wallace's administrative methods. Those methods had led to results that justified the important position he now held.

J. R. Beckett got down to work. He was beginning to feel the first symptoms of that almost religious fervor without which no great deed can be accomplished. He went over in his mind every detail of the information Mr. Jones had given him. He reread the note from the Cipher Section and the suggestions submitted by his colleagues. He felt they gave him nothing to go on for the moment. He put them carefully in order at the back of his mind and then purposely forgot all about them, knowing he would be able to recollect them the moment they could be of any use to him. He cleared all the papers off his table, except for the letter itself. This he began to read once again, slowly and out loud.

11

All freedom-loving people have a passion for conferences. The Negroes of Africa, the Chinese, the French, and the English are particularly keen on them. But the English give the word a special significance unknown to any primitive race. Their attitude toward a conference is fundamentally different. With them every item on the agenda is really and truly examined, and each member of the committee is separately invited to give his views. A conference is hardly ever attended by more than a dozen people. While each person in turn gives his opinion, the rest make a genuine effort to follow his argument, setting aside their own personal feelings in an attempt to understand the other's point of view. There is a pregnant silence at the end of each speech. When everyone has had his say, a decision is taken—invariably the one the discussion has revealed as being the most worth while.

In wartime a British conference assumed the solemn, almost religious, character of a secret-society meeting.

Conferences were held at every level of command, in the civil service as well as in the army. They were essential to the national character, for major decisions as well as for minor. Every time the British abstained from this preliminary spiritual communion or neglected any part of its ritual, there was an adverse repercussion throughout the Empire. The *Prince of Wales* would be sunk in the China Sea because the airmen who should have given her protection had dallied over an early-morning cup of tea; and not a single gun in the strongest naval base in the whole of the Far East could be trained so as to fire inland.

The Propaganda Minister himself, Sir James Middleton, presided over the conference at which Conrad submitted his scheme. Apart from the Minister, the secret committee that dealt with these questions consisted of four of his immediate colleagues, plus Gordon, as press representative, who had been invited to attend as Managing Editor of the most influential paper in the country.

In the course of his brief summary of the problem, Sir James said, "His Majesty's forces have undergone inevitable reverses on every front. In particular, the situation in the Far East—"

Everyone at once thought of the latest news from that part of the Empire. It was so depressing that Churchill had deemed it necessary to make a personal announcement and to give an explanation for the fall of Singapore without trying to conceal the important consequences of the disaster: the Japanese in possession of most of the world's rubber production, the rice crop in Burma, and the tin in Malaya; India and Australia threatened on both oceans; many thousands of our troops taken prisoner and abandoned to a fate worse than death. Conrad thought of Patton, and his heart gave a leap.

"This series of misfortunes," the Minister went on, "has obviously had an unfavorable effect on certain sections of the community. Following our usual practice, we have not suppressed any item of news, no matter how bad, so that today the Government is facing a certain amount of criticism. We know that final victory cannot be achieved without a number of heavy sacrifices, but in the meantime we must keep an eye on the morale of the nation. Now, recently there have been signs of alarm and despondency among the working and middle classes, and—strange as it may seem, gentlemen—most of all among the upper class, to which we have the honor to belong. This is not the general mood of the country, of course. So far, it is the exception rather than the rule. But it is nonetheless our duty to stifle any such pessimistic tendency at its source. That's a battle that has to be won at all costs. To conduct this battle we need men who are blessed with a combination of well-nigh contradictory qualities: pugnacity, psychological insight, and literary talent. Mr. Conrad, who will be addressing you shortly, is a man of this type. He is exceptionally distinguished not only as a soldier but also as a writer and journalist. He has had considerable experience of these matters abroad and has been able to study other methods besides our own. I'm sure you will all agree, gentlemen, that we could not have made a better choice."

A murmur of approval greeted this flattering introduction. Conrad let a minute or two go by, to give them time to digest Sir James Middleton's remarks, then embarked on his prologue in that odd foreign accent of his, which emphasized the originality of his text.

The silence that followed the first part of his address was not a sign of indifference but of deep concentration. It was broken at last by the Minister's private secretary, who said, "You know, there's certainly something in what you say."

"Something in what he says!" echoed Gordon. "I'd prefer to put it this way: What we've just heard makes more sense than all the balderdash printed in our newspapers for the last two years—with the exception of *Victory,* of course."

Sir James whispered to his secretary, "I must say, I'm most impressed by such a farsighted policy. This chap certainly knows what he's talking about, and knows how to put it across, too."

"That business about the one-eyed frog," mused Lord Godwin, the oldest member of the committee, "that certainly makes you think a bit!"

He was referring to an instance, based on biology, which Patton had once used to illustrate the influence of environment on the individual and which Conrad had worked into his text at the last moment, adapting it to the intellectual plane. He had felt this concrete example would have more effect on an audience that was possibly insensible to abstract ideas: "If you place a frog's egg in a solution containing certain chemical substances, the embryo will develop a single eye in the middle of its head instead of two on either side of it." Similarly, under the influence of ideas, the outlook of an individual mind could be altered. The aim of propaganda was to direct that outlook into useful channels.

The others said nothing, unwilling to commit themselves until they had heard what the scheme itself was to be. But their pensive silence bespoke an attitude that was by no means unfavorable. The Minister then summed up the general feeling of the meeting:

"I think we're all agreed on the principles you have outlined, Mr. Conrad. The proposal, as I see it, is to create a universal state of mind that will make even the damned Jerries convinced of our moral superiority, their own baseness, and the triumph of good over evil."

"Exactly. When we achieve that result, we shall have won the war."

This neat, epigrammatic statement was well received; the members of the committee showed their approval with a discreet smile.

"Now, gentlemen, let us consider Mr. Conrad's scheme for achieving this aim."

Conrad resumed his address. He knew how to underline the more important passages and bring certain details into sharper focus so as to present a vivid overall picture that kept his audience breathless with attention. The gentlemen were won over by his eloquence, and by the time he had finished speaking and offered to explain any point that was not perhaps quite clear, he knew he would encounter no serious opposition to his scheme.

"I always said this chap had more sense in his little finger than the whole of the Cabinet put together," Gordon muttered under his breath.

A lengthy discussion ensued, however. They were all anxious to justify the purpose of the conference, to make sure that no point had escaped them, and to show by their comments that they had clearly understood. Conrad had an answer ready for every question, and the clarity and vivacity of his replies that evening added considerably to his reputation. He throve on controversy, and having won his point was prepared to defend it verbally with arguments that he would not have dared commit to paper.

To Lord Godwin's doubt as to the possibility of changing, at this stage, the outlook of such a deeply fanatical nation as Germany by means of propaganda, however clever that propaganda might be, he replied by quoting certain statements made by Chancellor Adolf Hitler, as reported by Rauschning:

"Domination is inevitably the imposition of a strong will over a will that is weaker. What do I do to impose my will on an enemy? I first break and paralyze his own. I unsettle him and shake his self-confidence. . . . Foreign bodies then enter the enemy's blood stream, settle there, and produce a morbid condition, which eventually leads to a complete breakdown in the patient's resistance. . . ."

Conrad went thoroughly into this subject of propaganda aimed at the heart of the enemy. Lord Godwin's remark was very much to the point. It would indeed be a difficult and tricky undertaking. But there was no mind, however loyal to a particular ideal, that could not eventually be made receptive to the opposite ideal (the theories of the great German philosophers were, as usual, still uppermost in Conrad's mind). It was true that the German masses were fanatical and therefore impervious to a frontal attack. The Nazi party had been first in the field, and the masses' critical faculty had not been sufficiently developed to enable them to draw a comparison between the two doctrines. It was therefore necessary to resort to the artifice and subterfuge that Hitler himself had used when he took power and imposed himself on Europe. It was necessary to steer clear —this was another of the *Führer's* phrases—to steer clear of anything resembling argument or refutation, anything that offered an opening for discussion or doubt, and so beat the enemy with his own weapons. The corps of special agents whose formation Conrad advocated would operate, from the very start, not by means of open statements of fact but by suggestions and hints, by spreading seemingly inoffensive but cleverly thought-out rumors. This work would be carried out wherever the general public congregated: in shops, in the streets, in cafés and restaurants.

Sir James asked Conrad to give an example of what he meant. He did so.

"An agent could pretend to have heard from a friend of his who was a prisoner of war in England. He would make it known that this friend had no complaints, that he was being decently treated, that his rations were better than the *Wehrmacht* issue, and that no officer in captivity was obliged to work. These rumors would be repeated. They would be confirmed by other sources, by actual letters from a P.O.W. camp. People could always be found who were willing to write them; and besides, they would only be writing the truth. Another agent might claim to have a sister who was in England, married to an Englishman. He would describe how she was allowed complete freedom of movement; and her letters, dispatched via a neutral country, would express her sympathy for the wretched conditions in Germany and her regret at not being able to come to the help of her friends and relatives at home. Official broadcasts would add to the verisimilitude of these personal remarks, which, after all, would be completely accurate.

"Countless little pinpricks of this kind would gradually break down the people's resistance, so that finally a direct statement would have the desired effect on them. Victory would then be in sight. It simply requires patience, discretion, and cunning.

"In this country, on the other hand (Conrad did not mention England by name but simply said "in this country"—a manner of speech calculated to make a good impression on his audience, since they themselves and Churchill never used any other phrase when referring to England)—in this country, which has reached a higher state of evolution, there is no need to avoid positive statements when launching the campaign. The doctrine of human inviolability could not possibly shock anyone here."

The conference was drawing to a close. There was only one further objection, tentatively put forward by Lord Godwin, who seemed a little perturbed by the rather fascist character of this method of indoctrination. He did not care, he said, for conflicting moral values; and he felt there was a moral conflict between the form of this propaganda and its policy of individual freedom. What it came to, in fact, was the dissemination of liberal views by dictatorial methods—surely there was something rather objectionable in that?

Conrad felt exasperated to hear such ladylike over-refinement being voiced at such a critical hour. He was on the point of retorting, "Do you really think that in our case the ends don't justify the means?" but managed to choke back this Nietzschean principle and answered instead that he did not for a moment suggest adopting Fascist methods but that it would be criminally foolish not to take as much care in propagating the truth as the enemy took in distorting it.

The old gentleman was reduced to silence, and the rest of his colleagues succeeded in stifling any scruple they themselves might have had on that score. Conrad had infected them with his own enthusiasm. They were all completely won over by his scheme and eager to put it into operation. After a brief summing up, in which he thanked the speaker for his valuable suggestions, the Minister stated that the scheme would probably be adopted in its entirety and that special steps would be taken to hasten its being carried into effect. The meeting was then declared closed.

Conrad went home on foot, scarcely able to believe his success. He had almost arrived when a figure loomed up out of the fog and greeted him: "Good evening, sir." It was Mr. Malone, the hall porter.

"Good evening, Mr. Malone."

They walked side by side as far as the front door. Conrad had never been able to define what it was he found so disturbing about Mr. Malone. There was something odd about the man, something that gave rise in him to a feeling akin to nausea, and it disturbed him not to be able to fathom its cause. It was the sort of nausea, he imagined, that he might feel at the sight of some physical corruption or deformity.

Yet there was nothing freakish or deformed in the porter's outward appearance. Conrad reassured himself on this point once again by studying the man more closely. His height, his upright bearing, and discreet gestures betrayed nothing but a well-balanced personality and a sound constitution. Then why did he find his presence so disturbing that he always felt obliged to call him *Mr.* Malone?

"I've just been round to the club, sir. The missus is holding the fort."

So. Mr. Malone belonged to a club, just like a real gentleman. This thought suddenly dawned on Conrad, and in an instant he realized the reason for the strange impression the man's presence always made on him.

"The news isn't so good tonight, sir. We've lost Singapore."

The disturbing thing about him was simply his respectability. The strange impression he gave was due to the contrast between his social standing—his job as a porter—and his well-bred manners and habits. I should have noticed this ages ago, Conrad told himself. Mr. Malone did not behave like a porter, at least not like any of the porters Conrad had known in his youth, in Germany, Poland, and elsewhere in Europe. His suit was cut by a tailor who clearly knew his job. His trousers were beautifully creased. The overcoat he was wearing this evening might have belonged to Sir Wallace Goodfellow. But what Conrad found particularly striking, what he found disturbingly strange and outside all his previous experience, was the way in which the porter wore these perfectly conventional clothes, and the easy aristocratic manner he had, which was hardly at all different from that of a genuine peer. He's a distinguished-looking man, he said to himself, thinking how odd it was to arrive at this conclusion.

But it was true. Mr. Malone did look distinguished. Conrad wondered whether he was a rare exception or whether every hall porter in England bore the same stamp of personal dignity. He had had very little to do with the working class since his arrival in "this country."

"They say the bloody Japs are landing in Sumatra, sir."

There was nothing vulgar about his speech—just a trace of cockney accent where one might have expected incomprehensible slang. He used certain colorful expressions like "missus" and "bloody," but these cropped up barely more frequently than in upper-class conversation—perhaps even less so. Apart from this, he spoke exactly like a gentleman.

"Last month it was Rabaul in New Britain; now it looks as if it's going to be Australia next. I wonder what the American navy is doing, sir?"

Furthermore, he even thought like a gentleman. His natural reaction and concern was shared by everyone in the country who had heard Churchill's speech. Gordon's comment on the Japanese invasion had been much the same: "What the hell is the American navy doing?"

"What with Malaya and the Dutch East Indies, sir, they'll have almost all the rubber and tin in the world. And from Rangoon they're within striking distance of India. The Burma Road—"

He knew all about the resources of the Empire. He knew that Malaya was a producer of rubber and tin. He had studied maps of the Pacific and the Far East. He could tell where Australia, New Britain, India, and China lay in relation to one another. He was interested in this part of the world, which was so remote from his daily routine.

"The Chinese won't be able to check their advance along the Burma Road. They're creeping in everywhere like rats, sir, those bloody little yellow worms, just like rats or ants."

Here was another expression Conrad had heard before. It was Sir Wallace who the other day had angrily exclaimed, "Just like rats, those bloody little yellow worms!"

"We'll have to rely on our own forces to begin with, Mr. Malone," Conrad replied. "The American navy is still recovering from the lesson of Pearl Harbor. The Allies will rally round when they see how determined we are. It's not going to be easy, but we've won the main battle. At least the other fellows haven't managed to land here."

"I quite agree, sir. Hitler comes first. That's what the Old Man said—I listened to Churchill's speech, I can tell you. I'm sure he's right. But our poor chaps in the hands of those little yellow bastards are in for a pretty rough time."

They had reached the front door. Conrad quite naturally inquired after the health of Mrs. Malone, who suffered from regular bouts of rheumatism. The porter thanked him, and as he said good night assured him that all was well on that particular front.

12

"Here's our new *éminence grise,*" said Sir Wallace.

Conrad had come to fetch Lady Goodfellow, with whom he had promised to spend the afternoon visiting the wards.

"We've been hearing all sorts of things about you, my boy. It seems you're now to all intents and purposes Minister of Propaganda. I can't say I'm sorry. It's high time we had some young blood in Government circles."

Lady Goodfellow did not say anything, but the expression in her eyes betrayed unreserved admiration. Conrad tried to look surprised and pretended he had not understood.

"All right, all right, security above all, is that it? In that case I'll simply say that more men like you are needed, especially now the situation's going from bad to worse. If things go on like this, I honestly don't know what's going to happen. . . . Well, I must be off to the House, my dear. I'll leave you with our young friend here, and see that he's not led astray by some pretty little nurse. The country needs him, remember."

Sir Wallace went off, feeling a little more cheerful after this pleasantry. Conrad and Lady Goodfellow still showed no sign that they were on anything but strictly friendly terms.

"What's wrong with Sir Wallace today?" Conrad asked Lady Goodfellow. "He seems rather gloomy about the future."

"Oh, it's only the bad news that keeps coming in. All his friends are rather disheartened these days. Oh, darling, do you really think this war will ever end and that we'll come out on top? I'm beginning to be frightened by the news myself."

Conrad hastened to assure her that there was no doubt about the final outcome. Spontaneously, and much to his own surprise, he found himself repeating the arguments he had already used in countless articles, especially the ones he considered were most likely to appeal to this young woman's romantic side.

"If you had seen for yourself, as I have, the courage and tenacity of our men and the steadfast, confident leadership of our officers, you couldn't have any doubt about our ability to win. We've lost a few battles because we weren't sufficiently prepared, but no one will ever be able to break our spirit. Remember what Churchill said: 'What he has done is to kindle a fire in British hearts . . . which will burn with a steady and consuming flame until the last vestiges of Nazi tyranny have been burnt out.' "

"You know, darling, when you talk like that, it makes me feel much braver. If there were more people like you, our morale would be higher and everything would be much better. Only a moment ago Wallace was saying the same. He swears by you— But we'd better start if we don't want to be late. Will you help me with these parcels?"

She handed him some bags of candy and packages of cigarettes she had bought for the patients. As they were going out, she looked at his face and burst out laughing. "Oh, darling, my lipstick!"

He must have automatically brushed his lips against hers—an innocent habit that dated back to their first meeting in the hospital. He had been longing to kiss her ever since Sir Wallace had left the room.

She took out one of her last lace handkerchiefs to wipe his mouth, then changed her mind. Realizing perhaps that two flaws were as easy to repair as one, she gave him a second kiss, which, though well within the bounds of their platonic relationship, was nevertheless of slightly more consequence than the first. Then she wiped his mouth and they went off to cheer up the wounded.

Conrad did not care for these visits. He went only to please his companion. He hated being seen in civilian clothes, walking through the wards with a beautiful woman, and felt he could tell what the patients thought of him by the look in their eyes. Usually he never wore his decorations, but on these occasions he was careful to pin his M.C. to the lapel of his coat; and he instinctively exaggerated his limp.

The young Tank Corps corporal with whom Lady Goodfellow sat for a long time was no worse off than many of the others they had already seen. One of his legs had been amputated. He did not complain. Nor did he smile. There were no illusions in his mind as to what the future held for him.

Conrad felt a sudden surge of rage. He remembered having been similarly impressed, in a derisive and uncomprehending way, during one of the first actions in the war, when a young private in his company had had his arm taken off by a shell. That was the day he himself had won his medal. The citation mentioned his "leading the company in fierce hand-to-hand fighting, which was not called off until the enemy force had been completely wiped out." He tried to stifle his feelings with the thought that war was war and nothing could be done about it.

As they were leaving, Lady Goodfellow wiped away a tear. She was a genuinely tenderhearted woman who did her best to perform these acts of charity with as little fuss as possible. Conrad noticed she had the same dark circles under her eyes as Miss Barker. In addition to these daytime visits, Lady Goodfellow spent a whole night in the wards once a week and devoted hours of her spare time to knitting comforts for the troops.

"Darling," she whispered as she took his arm, "I know we're going to win the war, but how hard it's going to be! What we'll have to go through! What suffering and misery! Think of the number of young men crippled for life, like that one. We'll have to pay dearly for our victory. Couldn't we have found some way of avoiding all this bloodshed?"

But a veteran of the campaign in Flanders who was steeped in tales of manly exploit and heroic deed, even though in a fit of emotion he was sometimes moved to pity, would not hear of a nation being deterred from following the path of duty out of consideration for individual suffering. Conrad had been brought up on the doctrine of sacrifice and had been taught that the blood of martyrs was a necessary contribution to the glory of great nations. He remembered his mother and felt nothing but disgust for such faintheartedness. He could not bear to hear such thoughts being voiced by the lovely woman leaning on his arm, and impatiently turned on her.

"Have you ever thought of the price we should have to pay for coming to terms with a man like Hitler? Complete loss of liberty! National dishonor! And you dare to put that in the balance against a little transitory suffering! You're a fine example, I must say. We must remind ourselves every minute of the day, and remind the whole country, too, that what we're fighting for at the moment is nothing less than the continued existence of the world, an ideal whose attainment is of infinitely more importance than the fate of a single generation. We're in the forefront of the battle for the salvation of all humanity!"

He was carried away by his eloquence, impelled by the force of the arguments he had put forward a few days before. He tried desperately to find the right words, words that would have an effect not only on Lady Goodfellow herself but also, through her, on certain of her husband's colleagues whom he suspected of wavering—"a small minority in the governing classes," the Minister had said, "who are giving way to alarm and despondency."

"Have you also forgotten what Churchill said right at the beginning? 'I have nothing to offer but blood, toil, tears, and sweat. . . . You ask, What is our policy? I will say: "It is to wage war, by sea, land and air, with all our might.". . . You ask, What is our aim? I can answer in one word: "Victory." ' "

These words had sprung to his lips with such spontaneous sincerity that he felt deeply disturbed when he stopped to think about it. Lady Goodfellow acknowledged her disgrace. Leaning on his arm, she determined there and then never again to give way to such weakness and to do everything in her power to stifle any pessimistic tendency among her friends.

They finished their rounds a little earlier than they had expected. To show there were no hard feelings in spite of the lecture he had given her, Conrad suggested going to a movie. She gratefully agreed. They arrived in time for the last performance of the evening and had some difficulty in getting seats. There were queues at every box office.

Snowed under as he usually was by his work, Conrad had not been to a movie for a long time. At first he was rather bored by the film and could not disengage his mind from the welter of thoughts and emotions into which it was plunged. Subconsciously, he was shocked to find that an entertainment that drew such crowds was not being used for propaganda purposes, and his German conscience reproached him for this disloyal thought. Gradually, however, his interest was roused and he managed to become completely absorbed in the acting. The emotions he had experienced as a result of what he had seen and heard that day—the human misery of the hospital, Lady Goodfellow's remarks, and finally his own outburst—were all submerged in the last part of the film, in its final sequence of images and concluding bars of music, so as to produce a feeling of intensity bordering on tears, a combination of resentment, apprehension, and remorse.

Lady Goodfellow drew her hand away from his. The film was over. Every story leads up to a final climax, the epilogue of a book or a play to a climax only one degree less potent than sexual ecstasy or death.

The crowd rose to its feet and stood silently to attention as the last notes of the screen music were drowned by the opening bars of the national anthem.

"God save our gracious King . . ."

The crowd imperceptibly stiffened. The screen was suddenly flooded by a rectangle of light: a shimmering picture of King George. In this way two senses were satisfied instead of only one: sight, by the radiant image of the Sovereign; hearing, by the notes of solemn music surging up like a tidal wave.

"Long live our noble King . . ."

Gracious and noble—graciousness and nobility were successfully reflected in the eyes of the effigy on the screen.

"God Save the King."

This time there was no qualifying epithet, only the synthesis of a bare idea, an abstract figure—two symbols, four words, four waves of sound, one pair of eyes. The tension lifted as the verse and bar simultaneously came to an end. There was nothing more to be said.

"Send him victorious . . ."

Yes, there was still something. Once more the crowd had imperceptibly stiffened as the short silence was broken. The music started afresh, tugging at the heartstrings. On the screen, under the single eye of the crowd, the abstract figure began to fade, and the flags of the

Empire waving in the background could be seen quite clearly through it. The song of supplication had changed into a hymn of triumph: not triumph by brute force, but the inevitable, measured, majestic triumph of the abstraction on the screen. The beat of the music seemed to confirm his power, a power transcending all arms and armies, all war and warriors; a power rising above bloodshed and enmity. The abstraction was now almost completely submerged in the billowing waves of unfurled flags.

"Happy and glorious . . ."

There was a Latin harmony about this last word, an ancient consonance handed down from the past. The brilliant display on the screen combined into an apotheosis of happiness and glory. The music soared to ecstatic heights. The crowd was united in the single fellowship of joy. It was its odd capacity for joy that allowed this unimaginative nation to envisage a happy future for the abstraction.

"Long to reign over us . . ."

. . . and a future that was not even everlasting. The music swelled accordingly, to proportions that were vast but not eternal. The picture filled the whole screen, sharp and palpitating with life, its double symbol contained within strictly finite limits.

"God save the King."

The shimmering figure on the screen entered and melted the heart of the crowd, reducing the whole audience to a single composite mind. That was the first stage: the human stage. But it had not yet been completed; more time was needed for its evolution. When that was achieved, then perhaps eternity could be considered.

This time there was no more to be said. There remained only the repetition: a sequence of notes and the chorus taken up again with renewed intensity.

"Send him victorious . . . "

Repetition, cosmic force derived from a succession of impulses, was a known procedure, a procedure as old as music itself. Its effect was demonstrated by Joshua. When the walls of Jericho collapsed, they were simply paying tribute to the power of persistence.

For the second time that week William Conrad went through the delirious experience of a mystic revelation. His upbringing, or rather some characteristic handed down from his remote ancestors, made him susceptible to the influence of rhythmic display. As his own free will melted away, he felt himself seized heart and soul by the spirit of the crowd, the spirit of the crowd struggling desperately for existence in an infinity of possible combinations.

He was still capable—at least part of him was—of rational thought. That part of him, the reasonable and logical part, still retained sufficient self-control to criticize and condemn the enthusiastic counterpart. Who was it spoke of rationalist-enthusiasts? Patton had once mentioned them. Patton had described them, rather pedantically, as "the rationalists of the enthusiast class." He had used this term to define a specific category of individuals, whose numbers were negligible but whose existence could not be discounted, whose unexpected reactions could not be overlooked by the philosopher who wanted to elucidate certain historical incidents, any more than the existence and reactions of the "imp of the perverse" mentioned by Poe could be discounted or overlooked. The "rationalist of the enthusiast class" never lapsed into complete irresponsibility. He simply lost control of his emotions. Those emotions led to actions that reflected an inconsequent mixture of logic and madness.

"Happy and glorious . . ."

Those who belonged to this class remained clear-headed until they reached a state of delirium.

"Long to reign over us . . ."

The rationalist, on the other hand, would observe and try to analyze the penetrating power of the abstract figure, this fusion into a single mass of several separate masses. He would struggle to discover the reason for it, to draw comparisons, determine the analogy between it and the extravagant images palpitating in the mind of the enthusiast.

Determine the analogy. . . . That was Patton again, Patton describing the latest developments in modern science: disintegration, artificial radioactivity, the improvement made by a few French scientists on an abstract principle—another abstraction!—once expounded, and, Conrad added, by a dirty little German Jew—the bombardment of atoms by other atoms or atomic fragments. Under this bombardment, the atoms split—only a few to begin with—likewise projecting some elements of themselves against their neighbors, which in their turn exploded, unless their individual potential was sufficiently powerful to enable them to preserve their substance and structure intact. This operation could succeed only in the innermost core of the mass, for the individual potential was able to withstand a few isolated shocks. In scientific parlance, a "barrier of potential" was set up, and this protected the periphery against attack. But in the core of the mass, as soon as a few atoms had yielded, others in the immediate vicinity quickly succumbed under the devastating force of the explosion. The effective beaten zone soon became so wide that none could find protection. Then they all exploded, splitting into minute fragments—not always minute, however; the little Tank Corps corporal, for instance, had lost the whole of his leg; Miss Barker and Lady Goodfellow only the color in their cheeks; Adolf Hitler —but his mind was wandering.

Sympathetic detonations occurred right down the chain, link after link. Soon the whole mass was affected, its contents seething and boiling over. What happened next? Opinions varied on this point. Some spoke of transmutation, of base lead being changed into pure gold, of one kind of atom being transmuted into another. That, at least, was the theory put forward by the conservative-minded physicists. The biologists were equally modest in their claims. They spoke of mutation, of reptiles sprouting wings and developing feathers in place of their scales, or of primates growing human chins. Other scientists were more ambitious. They envisaged the complete annihilation of the atoms. If the operation were properly controlled, mass would be transmuted into energy.

"God save the King."

All this was still in the experimental stage. A definite conclusion had not yet been reached. The barrier remained intact. The possibilities were still unknown.

The fog began to lift. As soon as the music stopped, the fragmentary corpuscles were reintegrated into their several atoms as though the balance had been suddenly restored. After casting a final flashing beam, the effigy on the screen was extinguished. The spell was broken by the harsh glare of electric light. Minds and bodies were released from their state of tension. Backbones relaxed. Feet started moving. The rationalist was once again in control. The last waves of sound gradually subsided. Restored to their atomic state, the atoms began to flow in separate streams toward the various exits. Lady Goodfellow buttoned her gloves and murmured how much she had enjoyed the film.

13

Conrad's scheme was accepted in its entirety. Churchill gave his approval and decided to put it into operation at once. Working in the background, Conrad added a few finishing touches, supervised the mechanics of the task, and drafted some fresh suggestions, which were as dynamic as the original.

Each waking moment was devoted to this new mission of his. The authorities entrusted him more or less completely with the process of putting his brain child in working order. He was glad he had nothing else on his hands at the time, but even so he would never have got the job done without assistance. Miss Barker provided this assistance, silently, intelligently, efficiently. She had become his personal secretary now that Gordon had absolved her from her routine duties. Conrad was daily more and more delighted with her zeal for work, her orderly method, her filing system, her ability to put her finger on any document at a moment's notice and to remember even better than he could himself every detail of any draft he had made.

For several days they were hardly ever out of each other's sight. He allowed himself only a few hours' sleep every night, and without being asked she was almost as diligent in this respect as he was. She could only just bring herself to take an hour off in the evening to go out to have dinner with her airman. When that hour had elapsed, she came straight back to her desk, which was now installed in Conrad's office. The exact nature of their work was not known to the rest of the staff, who nevertheless divined its importance. Miss Barker's prestige was accordingly magnified.

They usually lunched together in the *Victory* canteen. Conrad enjoyed these meals as much as his outings with Lady Goodfellow. Encouraged by the interest he showed in her, Miss Barker had plucked up enough courage to tell him a little about her life. It was not particularly exciting, but he felt there was something rather touching about this humble career and was fascinated by all the little details of a world completely alien to his own.

Like Mr. Malone, Miss Barker had a modest background. She herself did not see how her commonplace experience could possibly be of any interest. She had been born in a little town on the south coast. Her mother was a washerwoman and had wanted to initiate her daughter into the British craft of laundering. Joan preferred reading. Her father, a veteran of the Merchant Marine who was paralyzed as a result of a sinking in icy seas during the First World War, drank more beer and whisky than was good for him; but in his sober moments he encouraged his daughter's natural inclination and occasionally gave her a few shillings to buy some books. Joan was fourteen when her parents died, within a few months of each other. She showed no particular emotion as she mentioned their deaths. After all, it was over and done with.

How could Conrad be bothered to listen to her account of what she went through when she found herself alone and almost penniless in London, living in a cheap bed-sitting room—until then she had lived with an elderly female relative, whom she had left on the spur of the moment after realizing, at the end of two years, how unpleasant and unbearable she was—and how she had overcome her despair and settled down to work all by herself, spending her last few pounds on a secretarial course? By a stroke of luck she had soon afterward got a good job in a bank. Many of her friends were less fortunate. Some had gone to the bad. Joan neither pitied nor envied them.

When war was declared, she had conscientiously listened to Churchill's speeches and to the young Princess Elizabeth's appeal to every woman in the country. She had thought it over and come to the conclusion that her job in the bank was scarcely commensurate with the total effort demanded of every British citizen. By a strange coincidence Gordon, who had met her in the bank, happened just then to be looking for a secretary. With his keen eye for order and efficiency—Joan did not tell him this herself, but Conrad knew it must have been the reason—he had offered her a job on the paper. At first she had not been able to make up her mind. Her idea at the time was to join up in one of the women's services. But Gordon had put it to her that she would be doing something far more worth while by working for a paper like *Victory* than for any military organization—here again Conrad could well imagine the scene—

so she had finally accepted. She had never regretted her decision. Gordon was a hard taskmaster but a kind man at heart, and the extra hours entailed in working for him had eased her conscience. The last pangs of regret she had felt at not being in uniform had vanished when she had been assigned to her present duties, for she was deeply conscious of their importance.

Joan was now earning enough to enable her to live in reasonable comfort, which she appreciated more than anything else. She had left her original bed-sitting room ages ago and now shared a comfortable place with a girl friend. Her airman was never allowed in there; if they spent the night together, it was always in some hotel bedroom. This was something else she did not reveal to Conrad, for fear of boring him with trivial details. She spoke about her boy friend quite openly and with no sense of shame; he was only a passing phase in her life. Conrad was therefore not a bit embarrassed.

They were sitting together at lunch one day, each with a tray containing a small piece of mutton, a few boiled potatoes, a little red currant jelly, a cup of tea, and a slice of bread, to which they had helped themselves from the self-service counter at the entrance. All round them other members of the *Victory* staff were solemnly doing justice to these rather meager rations.

At the next table there were two reporters who had recently joined the paper and whom Conrad did not know. They were having a heated discussion about the war. He found their chatter insufferable—just then he was trying to listen to Miss Barker, who was saying that at one stage in her life she would have thanked her lucky stars for a meal like this—but he could not help overhearing what they were saying, which he disliked even more.

"So this is what's known as lunch in this country nowadays. Look at this teaspoonful of jam; it's not enough to satisfy a babe in arms."

"And no butter, of course. It wouldn't be so bad if one had a decent breakfast in the morning. But what a hope! All the eggs are bought up by the bloated rich, the bacon goes to Buckingham Palace, and we haven't seen any porridge since the Germans started setting fire to the crops. I've just about had enough of this war. And what's it all for, that's what I'd like to know. Where is it going to get us in the end?"

Miss Barker had also overheard them; she had stopped halfway through her story.

"My car has just been requisitioned. I wish someone could tell me what possible military purpose a baby Austin can serve. For taking typists out on joy rides, I suppose. Meanwhile, seventy-ton German tanks are tearing our troops apart. Those chaps don't waste any time, I can tell you."

"Yes, you've got to hand it to the Nazis; they're miles ahead of us when it comes to organization. That fellow Hitler has certainly got something."

"The Yanks are only thinking of themselves, as usual. They'll wait till we're bled white before lifting a finger to help us. And of course the Russians are bound to do the dirty on us. I'm inclined to agree with the people who think we could have made a deal with Hitler. It's all so utterly senseless when you come to think of it. Do you really believe a few acres of Polish or Czechoslovakian territory are worth all this bloodshed? I ask you! Poland!"

The auditory organs receive an impression. The nervous system transmits this impression to the spinal cord. Nerve impulses are then sent from the spinal cord to the muscles, which automatically flex.

Conrad went for the reporter and knocked him down.

The rest of the nervous energy is relayed to the brain cells and there transformed into thought.

What atavistic instinct had ordained this behavior? What supernatural force had impelled Conrad, as once he had been impelled in his youth to knock down one of his friends who had been guilty of slacking? Could it be attributed to supreme artifice? Was the actor giving the finishing touch to the character he had assumed? The rationalist in him would not accept this as an excuse. He knew only too well that the real reason was to be found outside himself. It was the enthusiast who had taken control.

His hands were round the man's throat, and he was so enraged that he kept them there for some time without being able to utter a word. At last he broke out into a torrent of abuse against this cringing worm who called himself a man.

"I ought to have you arrested for talking like that. Rats like you ought to be strung up. They're a disgrace to the country. And just at this moment, when we're making the most gigantic effort in our history!"

Eventually Conrad managed to pull himself together, let go of his victim, who collapsed onto his seat, and went back, still trembling with anger, to rejoin Miss Barker.

Everyone in the place had stopped talking. Those who had overheard the conversation sided with Conrad. His outburst, which was against all the rules of gentlemanly behavior and self-control, was hardly considered in good taste; but it could be excused on the grounds of patriotic fervor, especially in the case of someone who had suffered so many hardships, including the misfortune of a foreign upbringing.

The incident was reported to Gordon in the course of the afternoon. He sent for the two reporters and dismissed them on the spot, after giving them both a dressing down that made them quake in their shoes. Then he went to Conrad's office to calm him down and apologize for the deplorable attitude shown by these two ex-members of his staff.

Conrad had just received another letter from Patton, sent before the fall of Singapore. Hearing from his friend had done something to relieve his feelings, but his gestures and expression still betrayed the disgust he felt. Gordon tried to pacify him with the assurance that everything was now all right, that this sort of thing would not happen twice, then left him with a friendly pat on the shoulder. As Gordon sat down at his own desk again, he shook his head in despair; and the new typist who had succeeded Miss Barker heard him muttering over and over again, "Really, these foreigners! These bloody, silly foreigners!"

14 Sir Wallace was reading Mr. Jones' latest report on G.Y.22.

"*15 February*. Submitted propaganda scheme at secret conference. Copy of scheme attached, with political section's comments. Conclusions: thoroughly good job, comprehensive and based on soundest principles. Shows wide experience, effort to cut red tape and get active results. Adoption of this scheme would benefit general conduct of the war. . . ."

This irritating opening paragraph provoked a caustic comment from Sir Wallace. "Oh, yes," he muttered, "the perfect pupil, exceptionally gifted, satisfactory in every respect!"

"*16 February*. Accompanied Lady G. on hospital rounds. Went with her to cinema. No fresh developments."

Sir Wallace stopped reading for a moment and blinked—the only outward sign of his irritation—and then went on.

"*Note:* Propaganda scheme adopted *in toto*. Action taken, with G.Y.22 unofficially responsible for supervision of details. Now absorbed in this task, working all day and night in newspaper office. Miss B., now his personal secretary, always with him. Lunch every day together in canteen. Miss B. still sees Flight-Lieut. W., but only occasionally, when work permits. Never mentions nature of her present assignment, naturally enough.

"*24 February*. Violent scene during luncheon in canteen."

Sir Wallace studied the detailed account of the fight and began thinking. Was it reasonable to imagine such behavior on the part of a spy? Was it possible to go to such lengths as to imitate blind fury? To pretend to lose all self-control in a transport of passion? Well, it was not impossible. "Yet it doesn't seem likely," he grudgingly muttered.

"Miss B. described the scene to Flight-Lieut. W., betraying much admiration for the behavior of G.Y. 22.

"*Same day*. Received a letter from Captain A.P., a regular correspondent. See copy from Censor. No comment."

After this Mr. Jones had left a large gap, to show that the subsequent information was not part of the main report; and to make this still clearer, he had started the next paragraph with the word "BUT," typed in capital letters. Sir Wallace was pleased with this graphic exposition.

"BUT

"1. Duncan reports additional detail ref. Report No. 7. The evening of 12 December, when G.Y.22 received letter from unknown admirer (now in hands of J. R. Beckett), he betrayed abnormal emotion. Contrary to his usual habit, he failed to correct typescript of an article and left the office *in great haste*.

"2. J. R. Beckett reports he is definitely on to something, but cannot yet give a specific opinion."

Sir Wallace gave a whistle of surprise, then in his normal voice shouted for Mr. Jones. Mr. Jones appeared in a flash. He was expecting this summons.

"Jones," he began, carefully weighing his words, "I should like to know how Duncan came across this information."

There was no need for him to be more explicit; Mr. Jones understood at once.

"I suppose he interrogated Flight-Lieutenant W. again, sir, on some point he had not got quite clear before."

As he gave this reply, Mr. Jones stood to attention as rigidly as Nelson's Column. Sir Wallace, who was observing him closely, felt there was something odd about his manner. He went on, "Yes, Jones, I suppose that was it. And you've no idea, of course, what could have prompted him to put his questions in such a way as to make the answers yield a fresh detail, an important detail, which had not been disclosed before?"

Mr. Jones' features were frozen in an expression that might easily have been taken for sheer stupidity.

"Well, sir, perhaps Duncan realized you're particularly interested in this case. When I saw him the other day, I made it quite clear that you still demanded a continued effort, from which he was not to be deterred by the face value of the case. In fact, sir, I went so far as to tell him that G.Y.22 *was* an enemy agent and that without giving anything away you insisted on his being considered as such. I felt it would be in order to go to those lengths, sir."

Sir Wallace smiled. Mr. Jones remained inscrutable.

"And no doubt Flight-Lieutenant W. suddenly remembered something Miss B. had said—something he'd forgotten up till then? No doubt he cleverly encouraged her to give him a little further information? No doubt he was prompted to do this by something Duncan had told him? Don't you think so, Jones?"

"It's quite possible, sir. I didn't think there was any need to question him on that point."

"That's all right, Jones. You can see for yourself now that we mustn't leave a single stone unturned, or ever be afraid of exposing ourselves to ridicule. Never admit defeat, Jones; that's a lesson we've all got to learn. And what did Beckett say exactly?"

"No more than what's in my report, sir. Considering the rather special nature of his work, I didn't pursue the inquiry any further. But as a result of Duncan's report, and since you were away at the time, I felt I should let him know that our suspicions were founded on actual fact. Two days later, sir, he told me he thought he was on to something."

"Well done, Jones. I believe we're getting somewhere at last. Beckett's anything but a line-shooter. If he told you that, then there must be something in it. Otherwise, he wouldn't have said anything at all."

"I quite agree, sir."

"Well, there's nothing more we can do at the moment. But what do you think about the canteen scene, Jones?"

"Rather puzzling on the face of it. I've been thinking about it quite a lot, sir."

"And what conclusions have you reached?"

"Well, sir, I don't think it gives us any reason for changing our present attitude. If G.Y.22 really is a Nazi agent, from what we've seen of his behavior up till now he's quite obviously a first-class man at his job. I feel this latest incident only confirms his devilish cunning, his remarkable coolness, which enables him to turn everything to his own advantage. From the facts as we know them, he seems to be following a specific policy, which is to prove his loyalty to this country on every possible occasion. Perhaps he's being held in reserve for some really important operation. No doubt he has been briefed never to overlook a single opportunity for making a show of patriotism, and he has taken his briefing to heart. That conversation in the canteen happened to be a perfect opportunity, and naturally he jumped at it. He made up his mind in a split second; and his performance, I'm sure you'll agree, sir, was pretty well perfect. An astounding combination of decision and acting ability. He's a genius in the part he has been given to play, sir, and for that reason all the more dangerous."

Sir Wallace was rather impressed by his assistant's summing up and kept turning it over in his mind.

"Yes, Jones, you're probably quite right. A first-class actor, cool as a cucumber. . . . And yet that fight—Well, never mind, we'll soon see what's behind it all. All right, Jones, I shan't be needing you for the moment. I'll just have a look at our philosopher's latest effusion. That might give me something to think about. Did you find anything interesting in it?"

"From a certain point of view, sir, yes; though it has

nothing to do with the case itself. What I mean is, I believe the writer's perfectly innocent, and there's a lot of sense in what he says. I've read all his letters pretty carefully."

"You may be right, Jones," he replied, trying to keep a straight face. "In our job there's always some lesson to be learned."

Mr. Jones disappeared into the room next door, and with a sigh of resignation Sir Wallace began reading Patton's latest letter:

"My dear William,

"I'm back in Singapore, in the same camp from which first I wrote you. This reminds me of the coercive influence of environment.

"I believe I told you that sense of unity was much in evidence in this part of the world. Is this a sign of socialism, I wonder? If so, we're probably closer to socialism than any other nation in the world. You only have to look at any community outside the British Isles, particularly in Europe, which you know far better than I do: As soon as one of its members opens his mouth, all the rest feel embarrassed. The constitution of our community system explains why the average Englishman never feels obliged to think. The collective spirit absolves him more or less completely from this mental process, since it does all his thinking for him. Being relieved of this responsibility, which is taken on by the community, he has more time to concentrate on cricket, which is more his line. What I've seen of the army has only served to confirm me in this view. Does that mean we're turning into a nation of robots? I don't think so. After all, we still pride ourselves on our love of liberty. It's not incompatible. As

you know, every atom is individually free and unfettered. But once it is joined by others, it comes under common law. The connection between the tangible universe and the universe beyond our senses is closer than most people think."

"I'll never be able to understand why this chap can't talk reasonably like anyone else," grumbled Sir Wallace. "Why can't he put two sentences together without dragging the universe into his argument?"

"You've probably heard it said that individually we're charming but, as a nation, unbearable. That's the opinion of people for whom cricket means more than abstract thought, and there's something to be said for it. Shaw considers us from every point of view elementary, puerile, and stupid. But even though he has realized the truth of creative evolution, even though he has managed to avoid the pitfalls of romanticism and can talk quite naturally about natural laws, even he hasn't enough imagination to envisage successive emergence except on the individual plane. He will probably die without ever being aware that, collectively speaking, we've already reached that state of maturity that, according to him, won't be reached by the individual before 31920 A.D. The very existence of community thinking escapes this socialist. He sees nothing but cricket and fox hunting, and despises both. He mistakes division of labor for absence of labor. He must be blind not to be able to see that in England all thought is the responsibility of the community. And since thought is abstract, and so is the community, the concrete work is entrusted to the artisan. Consequently, we're much better off than most

people, besides constituting an almost perfect collective whole. . . ."

"Very clever, I'm sure," Sir Wallace remarked.

"I forgot to tell you—I should have started with this, but you've probably guessed it already—that my own environment at the moment is not exactly normal. I've just come back from up north with my company, almost as far as Penang. At last I've seen the jungle, quite a few plantations, one or two golf courses, some Chinese, Hindus, and Malayans, and any amount of Japanese aircraft. The R.A.F. was conspicuous by its absence—late as usual—but we must be patient, I suppose. Well, we kept marching north until we came up against the Japanese; then we about-turned and came straight back here. The return trip took slightly longer than the outward journey, but there wasn't much in it. Following his usual habit, Tommy Atkins has started this battle with a withdrawal of several hundred miles. I should love to know what 'idea' accounts for such a universal law as this. . . ."

"This chap has got an absolute passion for ideas," muttered Sir Wallace.

"Perhaps in our case it's a yearning for fresh experience, the experience of getting out of a tight hole in the jungle? Or did we instinctively make for Singapore simply because we only feel at home when surrounded on all sides by water? Whatever the reason, we got back here yesterday evening, with the Japs on our heels, and were given twenty-four hours in which to rest and tidy up. I'm taking advantage of this to write a few lines, hoping they will reach you sometime. We're no longer retreating, because the sea is just behind us—but joking apart, things aren't so bad

really. Most of our troops have withdrawn to the island of Singapore, and, as you know, there's not much we don't know about defending islands. So there's still some hope. . . ."

"You're telling me!" growled Sir Wallace.

"I still can't help thinking about the Old Goat. I feel irresistibly drawn towards him, even now. From time to time, even in this country, some original character appears on the scene, someone who tries to be something more than the mere reflection of the communal mind. As long as his efforts are confined to abstract thought, we let him have his way; in fact the community may even benefit from them, for no one can deny there's always room for improvement. But if this eccentric is tempted to take action, to put his ideas into practice, then the community is sufficiently wise and sufficiently powerful to make it impossible for him to do any harm, while still respecting him for making the attempt. Edward VIII, for instance, was soon brought to book. The Old Goat would have given us far less trouble than he did; at least he has never had the wild idea of marrying an American.

"This quality of originality, which the Old Goat shares with a few others, is simply a manifestation of Art. Don't think that's a contradiction in terms. Instead of creating, that's to say interfering with the forces of nature, Art almost invariably distorts and is therefore destructive. It's an unhealthy and essentially individual reaction against communal life. Creative artists, genuine artists, are the greatest enemies of our country and of humanity as a whole. We instinctively recoil from them as we would from the plague. Our poets are not creative artists in the Continental sense

of the word. They're philosophers. Wilde was criticized for The Picture of Dorian Gray, *a book that is incapable of corrupting anyone but that might be regarded as a glorification of the artist's creative faculty. In the Old Goat's case artistic mania has assumed its most dangerous form. His object is to refashion the community. The community has got its own back by twisting his original ideas round to such an extent that even he is probably now unable to recognize them. What he first conceived as a biological law, as evolution and progress, has since been reduced by the masses to the massacre of millions of Jews. What he first regarded as the power of the word, as the propagation of the Ideal, the masses have degraded to concentration-camp and Gestapo level. He dreamt of the triumph of the mind; the masses have interpreted his dreams in terms of brutal conquest. The masses could not have done otherwise; it was madness on his part to try to put his ideas into practice in the first place. Subsequently, he was obliged to accept these distortions and even adopt them, since he prided himself on his ability to dictate history. All he could do then was declare that these pogroms, concentration camps, and war were inseparable from his doctrine and essential to the fulfillment of his ideal. He said this so loudly and so often that he finally came to believe it himself —quite a common form of autosuggestion, which shouldn't surprise anyone.*

"Well, old boy, I must stop now. I only hope I haven't bored you too much. If you like, you can put it all down to my recent trip up north and back again under a tropical sun. You can also blame malaria a little. I haven't had a letter from you for ages. But

I've heard about you indirectly from a friend, who tells me you're now a very important person—a Ministry adviser or something of that sort. I'm glad to hear it, though I can't say I'm surprised—either at you, because I always knew you were too good to remain a captain for long, or at our ministers, because they're always on the lookout for some competent fellow to do their work for them. It's from us that the Americans have inherited the art of making proper use of technical personnel. Anyway, drop me a line sometime, if only to keep the censors busy. They'll have some fun with this letter, all right. That's why I've written it.

"All the best,

"A. Patton."

"Well!" Sir Wallace heaved a sigh of relief. "Thank God that's over. And Jones finds it all quite interesting! Thank heavens those 'trips' of his through the jungle don't allow him to write every day. I wonder what has become of him now, the wretched brute?"

15

J. R. Beckett was hard at work.

A detailed study of the letter had encouraged him to persevere in his efforts. A good deal of ground had been covered since the day the Cipher Section had handed the document over to him.

The specialists who had tried in vain to decipher it before him had made the following comments: "If the letter contains a hidden message, it is most likely based on one of the *N* codes. The length of the letter justifies this assumption, but there is nothing to lead one to suppose that it actually does contain a hidden message."

J. R. Beckett fully agreed. But since his interest had been thoroughly aroused, he interpreted his colleagues' remarks in the following manner: "If the letter contains a hidden message, it is probably based on an *N* code. Now, the letter does contain a hidden message; therefore it must be based on an *N* code."

The principle of *N* codes is known to every cipher expert. Its advantage lies in its ability to conceal in an apparently innocuous letter not only a secret message but the actual presence of a secret message.

The coding process usually consists of two stages:

1. Each of the letters of the message to be coded—this code can be used only for a fairly short message; otherwise it entails an inconveniently long communication—each of the letters of the message to be coded is made to correspond with a certain number.

This preliminary operation is a classic procedure, and its variations are unlimited. Substituting *1* for *a*, *2* for *b*, and so on would obviously be considered rather too simple by the masters of epistolary esotericism. One of the procedures most in use, which is easy and relatively foolproof, is to agree in advance on a certain passage of a certain book, more often than not a dictionary, since a dictionary is also required for the second stage. Supposing the first letter of the message to be a *d*, the sender would pick out the first *d* in the selected passage; supposing this *d* to be the twelfth letter of the second line, then the number corresponding to it would be *212* (second line, twelfth letter). There is an alternative method, in which the line number is not included in the final figure but the number of letters from the beginning of the passage is counted instead. In the example above, if the first line contained 42 letters, the first *d* would therefore be the fifty-fourth letter, and so the number corresponding to it would be 54. This operation is then repeated for every letter in the message.

When this stage is completed, the whole message is transformed into a series of numbers. An amateur might be content to stop there, believing that this sequence of numerals would defy the ingenuity of anyone unacquainted with the selected book and the specific passage in it. This point of view would amuse the experts, who know that cryptograms of this type are only too easy to solve—easy for various reasons, but chiefly because a series of numbers at once betrays the *presence* of a secret message; and once the presence of a secret message is revealed, the message itself can be very quickly brought to light.

But by means of the second operation, fruit of a mastermind, this series of figures can be changed into a sequence of words, *and in such a way as to leave a sufficiently wide choice so that each of these words can be inserted, with a little imagination, into an innocuous and perfectly coherent letter.*

> 2. The sender and recipient having both agreed in advance on a certain dictionary, preferably an edition in common use such as the *Pocket Oxford,* and supposing the number to be changed into a word is 212, the sender turns to *page 212* in the dictionary and picks out *any* word that appears on that page—"delay," "delegate," "delight," or "deliver," for instance—any word that falls most naturally into the text of the letter he proposes to write. The choice of word, in fact, is only partly dictated; to use a mathematical term, there is a certain *degree of freedom.*

The rest of the operation is a fascinating game in which the sender can allow his imagination and ingenuity full rein. He makes a rough draft, writing down the words corresponding to the numbers making up the coded message, but leaving a gap between them—for of course it is also agreed in advance that each of the key words should be separated from its neighbor by a given number of "loose" words, or "plug." He then composes his letter in such a way that the key words fall quite naturally into the context. This task may take several hours before a satisfactory result is achieved. Very often it is necessary to begin all over again. If a word looks at all artificial in context, for instance, another word from the same page of the dictionary may have to be substituted. As the number of the page remains constant, however, the sense of the concealed message would not be altered by this substitution. A cleverly composed letter of this kind had every chance of passing unnoticed.

J. R. Beckett had started off by basing his investigation on the following *a priori* argument:

G.Y.22 was an enemy agent—that was the basic assumption—who after several years' residence in this country had won, by virtue of his ability and patience, a position of importance above all suspicion. His chiefs were now anxious to get in touch with him without using a direct contact, direct contacts always being a danger. The accomplice who had been detailed to approach him would therefore not be allowed to do so directly. This was one of the most elementary rules of the game.

J. R. Beckett now put himself in the accomplice's place. He would probably say to himself, All letters are read by the censor, or are at least open to censorship. I have no connection with this writer—a fact that is probably known. I have no wish for any future connection with him—that, too, is one of the most elementary rules of the game. So I must find some pretext for sending him a letter that neither presupposes nor leads to any connection between us. The most obvious pretext, in view of the recipient's profession, would be a tribute from an unknown admirer to a famous author. Considering the glamour that always surrounds an author, this admirer would more likely be a woman than a man—perhaps a dear old maid with rather romantic notions.

Having reached this point in his reasoning, J. R. Beckett read the letter over again and came to the conclusion that most of the phrases in it justified his assumption that the writer was posing as a dear old maid with rather romantic notions. Obviously, there was no logical proof—just because highly seasoned food was capable of disguising the taste of poison, there was no reason to suspect the presence of poison in every curry—but all the same he felt he was on to something.

Starting from this *a priori* argument, J. R. Beckett struck out blindly in the dark.

To follow his progress and try to describe it would be an arduous and thankless task. A whole volume would scarcely suffice to account for the many trains of thought he embarked on, pursued, and then abandoned. He followed his usual habit of moving from the general to the particular, forming an impression of the whole before studying the detail, seizing on the atmosphere, which, however superficial and misleading, might still act as a valuable signpost, before examining the facts, paying as much attention to the form as to the content.

One result of this work had been to reveal a difference in style between the first part of the letter and the final sentences. The letter started off, for instance, with the following passage:

"I have read all your books with passionate interest

and feast on your articles every week. At my age, and living alone, I find these an enormous consolation. I am enchanted to see you expressing so admirably exactly what I feel myself, and fighting for an ideal I value highly. God will surely reward you for contributing to His cause a talent as rare as yours. . . ."

Here there was a logical sequence of ideas. The style was faultless, even fairly elegant, and betrayed a certain degree of literary taste. If J. R. Beckett's assumption was correct, the sender of the message must have made a real effort to produce such a coherent and consecutive result. Toward the end of the letter, on the other hand, there was this:

"I should very much like to make your acquaintance. This terrible and tiresome blockade will not dampen our wonderful ardor, and there is no doubt the years will bring sweet consolation. We'll rise from this abyss and soon see our splendid aircraft liberating our beautiful and beloved country. . . ."

Comparison of this passage with the initial sentences set J. R. Beckett tingling with anticipation.

J. R. Beckett now embarked on a detailed study.

He began by analyzing this second passage, which occurred toward the end of the fourth page—the letter was five pages long—in the first place, because it stuck out a mile; and in the second place, because of a more general reason: In the initial stages of a composition of this kind, the sender would have all his wits about him. His ingenuity would be stimulated by the interest and amusement he felt in the work; he would therefore make it as perfect as possible and use no word that might rouse suspicion. But this task sometimes took several hours and required intense concentration. The initial enthusiasm would give way to fatigue and boredom. The task could not be put off till the following day—J. R. Beckett was well aware that in this kind of work essential rough drafts were never kept overnight before being destroyed, even in the most secure hideout. Thus the human element came into it, and the end of the letter was often knocked off rather hastily. When the sender was not at the top of his form, the inclusion of the key words imposed a strain on the sense of the letter and the style of the writing. Nor was it possible to avoid this by composing the end of the letter first, for the key words were not inserted throughout the text. The message ended at a specific point, indicated by a code sign, but the letter itself would go on for several more lines of "plug." This was yet another of the elementary rules of the game.

"I should very much like to make your acquaintance. This terrible and tiresome blockade will not dampen our wonderful ardor, and there is no doubt the years will bring sweet consolation. We'll rise from this abyss and soon see our splendid aircraft liberating our beautiful and beloved country. . . ."

On the basis of these few lines J. R. Beckett formed a general impression and made a number of particular notes. His impression was that the phrases were badly strung together, the style flat and uninspired, too free a use being made of commonplace epithets, meaningless adjectives. This did not surprise him at all. It was what he expected, or rather what he was hoping for. There was no reason to suppose that a secret agent was infallible, even a German secret agent.

The particular notes consisted of a detailed, itemized analysis of his general impression:

"1. 'This terrible and tiresome blockade.' The sequence of these two epithets is neither logical nor even natural in a writer who is capable of expressing herself clearly and with a certain amount of elegance, as she has shown at the beginning. 'Tiresome' after 'terrible'? 'This terrible blockade' would have been quite enough and would have sounded more natural. . . . But here, what's this? Here's something more unnatural still. I hadn't noticed it before, yet it stands out a mile! A real bloomer! A foreigner might talk about a blockade, but certainly not an Englishwoman. After all, Britannia rules the waves! A blockade has never been heard of in this country. It's a bad slip, an inevitable slip on the part of someone so mentally exhausted as to let herself be ruled by her instinct.

"2. 'Wonderful ardor,' 'there is no doubt,' 'sweet consolation.' Platitudes. Clichés. Vulgarity.

"3. 'We'll rise from this abyss.' 'Abyss' is completely artificial, absolutely unconnected in feeling with the phrase immediately preceding it. A blockade does not evoke the picture of an abyss. Furthermore, this word seems strangely pessimistic after the note of confidence struck in the first part of the letter.

"4. 'Our splendid aircraft.' Another trite epithet. And why the air force in preference to any other service? Why not 'our glorious army'? For that matter, why not 'our invincible navy,' seeing that it's supposed to be an Englishwoman speaking on the subject of blockades?

"5. 'Liberating our beautiful and beloved country.' In the first place, the country isn't in chains. It's the writer who appears to be chained to the idea evoked by the use of the word 'blockade.' Secondly, more epithets! Nothing, not even patriotic fervor, can possibly justify 'beautiful' in this particular context—except, of course, the need to fill a gap.

Having put down on paper the details of his general impression, J. R. Beckett settled down to consider them.

His aim during this initial stage was to pick out the words with a double meaning, the key words, which were partly dictated, from the intermediary "plugs," which were left to the writer's imagination. Most of his colleagues would have worked on the following assumption: "Phrases such as 'there is no doubt,' 'sweet consolation,' 'beautiful country,' etc., which seem out of place in someone who writes reasonably well, have most probably been dictated by the limited choice of words provided by single pages of the dictionary. It is these phrases, therefore, that are most likely to contain the key words."

But J. R. Beckett had not reached his present high rank by working on the same principles as his colleagues. In this case, for instance, he had formed an opinion that was diametrically opposed to theirs. His argument was: "It is just because these trite phrases stand out a mile that they cannot possibly contain the key words." It would be tedious to outline all his reasons for coming to this conclusion, but this was one he considered particularly cogent: "If these really are the key words, then precisely because they are so trite, any fool, no matter how tired he was, could have made them fall quite naturally into sentences making more sense and composed in a better style than the passage in which they actually appear. In fact, they do not affect the style or the sense in any way. They are simply 'plugs.' Clearly, then, the key words are to be found elsewhere. The sender obviously got tired and simply filled in the gaps with the first thing that came into his head without bothering to think whether it makes good sense or not."

Having come to this conclusion, J. R. Beckett got out a pencil and a fresh sheet of paper and started feeling his way.

After countless efforts, after embarking on several lines of thought only to abandon them one after the other, he reached a definite verdict, the only verdict that seemed completely incontrovertible. It was this: "The key words in the passage under consideration are the following—'blockade,' 'ardor,' 'doubt,' 'consolation,' 'abyss,' 'aircraft,' and 'beloved.' "

"These words are separated by alternate sequences of four and five 'plug' words, the whole forming a chain made up of two separate series of links, as is frequently the case in this type of cryptogram, *i.e.*, key word, four 'plugs,' key word, five 'plugs,' and so on."

J. R. Beckett then considered these words as a whole and made a fresh discovery, which was "sweet consolation" indeed, namely that all the words he had picked out had a common characteristic: They all started with one of the first four letters of the alphabet, with *a, b, c,* or *d*.

Now, in the popular editions of most dictionaries, words with this characteristic were generally to be found within the first three hundred pages. And since, during the first stage of an *N* code, each letter of the message was transformed into a three-digit number, the first digit being the number of the line in the specific passage where that letter appeared for the first time, it was obvious that the letter in question, unless it happened to be one that was extremely rarely used, would be found in the first or second line of the passage—in other words, that the number corresponding to it would be more often than not less than 300; *i.e.*, the first figure would be either *1* or *2*, or, to put it another way still, the first letter of the key word would be either *a, b, c,* or *d.* The fact that this actually was so did not constitute a positive proof—J. R. Beckett denied the very existence of positive proofs—but it did lend additional support to the conviction that was gradually taking shape in his mind.

J. R. Beckett continued to follow this trail. Working backwards, then forwards, from the passage he had analyzed, he finally determined all the words he believed to be key words according to his assumption that the chain consisted of two regular series of links. And he discovered that every one of them, with a few rare exceptions, had *a, b, c,* or *d* as its first letter.

At this discovery J. R. Beckett smiled, and in spite of the austere drink restrictions poured himself out a double whisky and soda. It was then that he gave Mr. Jones the hint in which Sir Wallace had seen a faint ray of hope.

He was still hard at work, but there remained a great deal of ground to be covered. Thinking of the various possible ways and means of reaching his goal all the more quickly, he scribbled a short note on a piece of paper: "Please let me have complete list of dictionaries kept in G.Y.22's flat, with dates of publication," and went out to deliver it himself at the address which Mr. Jones had given him.

Author's Note: In a narrative in which the methods, the ways and means, of tackling and solving a problem are of almost equal importance as the characters themselves, the author has not seen fit to pass over in silence the various mental processes of the modest and useful gentleman known as J. R. Beckett. For the most part, however, he has tried to confine himself to basic principles, deeming it superfluous to give more than a rough outline of this method and procedure. He therefore craves the reader's indulgence should this brief summary appear either too detailed or else not sufficiently complete.

Morover, the mind of this modest gentleman occasionally functions in such an erratic manner that it would be impossible to make a note of all the subsidiary ideas that branch out from his main train of thought. Here, for instance, is one of these mental offshoots, intentionally omitted from the text as being of only secondary importance in itself but which nevertheless could lead to results of the greatest consequence.

In examining the letter, J. R. Beckett found that a very high proportion of the key words began with the letters *do, dr,* and *du*. Generally speaking, these words occurred well within the first three hundred pages of any popular dictionary, but certainly not right at the beginning. In most editions they would be found between pages 200 and 300; a few might be found even after page 300; fewer still, but these were real exceptions, between pages 100 and 200, in which case, however, they would almost always occur after page 140 or 150. The message therefore contained a very high proportion of letters that did *not* occur in the first line of the selected passage, or that occurred only at the very end of this line, assuming it consisted of more than forty letters.

But the most commonly used letters are almost always found in the first line or in any other line of a given passage, provided these lines are of normal length. In this case the fact that *some* of the letters did not fall into this general category would have been of no particular significance, but the fact that a *very high proportion* of them formed an exception to the rule was an anomaly that could not be disregarded. A possible explanation for this—possible but by no means certain—was that in this particular case the first line of the passage was very short—perhaps a half line, *such as occurs at the end of a paragraph;* though it was only an assumption that the selected passage did begin with such a line.

Here was a discovery that was of no immediate use but that might prove to be an extremely valuable clue when it came to unearthing the famous passage itself, a clue that could be added to the countless others that were already stored in J. R. Beckett's memory, which the author will leave for the time being in their latent undeveloped state.

16 SURABAYA

"My dear William,

"My last two forecasts were both wrong: The sea did not check our withdrawal farther south; and we failed to hold our island. It was too close to the mainland.

"I managed to get out of Singapore with some of my company the day after the capitulation; we escaped in an old sailing ship. It was Dunkirk all over again, but on a smaller scale. It looks as if we shall have plenty of embarkation experience by the time we're ready to 'disembark.'

"It was one of the most interesting episodes of the glorious campaign, and I would not have missed it for anything—a leaky old Chinese junk with a lateen sail in shreds, not even white but earth-colored, with the Jocks and myself disguised as mandarins in huge pointed hats. The Japanese navy turned their noses up at us; so did their air force. It took us eight days to

get to Sumatra. From there, as the Japs were still advancing by sea as well as on land, we were sent still farther south, to Java, where I am at the moment. Perhaps they'll try and make us defend this island as well; or perhaps we'll be sent to Australia; I don't know yet. But I'm delighted with all this traveling.

"I hope you people at home aren't too disheartened by the way things have turned out over here. It won't be long before we win back all the ground we've lost —just as soon as the Old Goat is brought to his senses concerning the laws of nature, which is bound to happen sometime. There's a rumor, which has reached us even in this part of the world, that you're actually engaged on this task—is it a secret? sorry!—so you see, we're not really so out of touch with things as some people seem to think. Do drop me a line when you have a moment to spare: 'Major Patton, B.A.P.O. 63.' Yes, I'm a major now, thanks to that little cruise. Utterly unfair, of course; I should have been made an admiral.

"No more for now. I'll try and write a longer letter next time. Till then, all the best.

"A. Patton

"P.S. *As you're in the know, perhaps you can tell me what the hell the bloody American navy is doing?"*

This letter had taken over a month to arrive. Conrad felt deeply relieved and hoped that the next lot of news from his friend would be slightly more up to date.

Ever since the day he lost his temper and punched a British subject on the nose for grousing in public, William Conrad had tried to keep his feelings under control by putting all he had into his work and making every effort to combat alarm and despondency. Day by day the character he had assumed became more and more deeply engulfed by the mission in hand.

Apart from his semiofficial functions he still led an active social life, making his mark in a variety of circles by his conversation no less than by the example he set. Thanks to the Goodfellows, every door in London was open to him. Lady Goodfellow repeated his remarks, which on her lips sounded all the more forceful; and in her own behavior she provided a standard of conduct that was an inspiration to all her friends. Having once caught her husband drinking his favorite liquor, she made him feel ashamed by quoting a few of Conrad's statements. Grinding his teeth, burning inwardly with rage, Sir Wallace listened with a pitiful air of contrition. He had to yield. He heroically put an end to his nightly debauch and instead invested the money he used to squander on black-market whisky in national savings certificates. Among his friends and parliamentary acquaintances, the baronet never stopped singing the praises of the new apostle and was busy pulling strings at a high level to get him awarded the George Cross—a negligible recognition, he claimed, for such a loyal servant of the country.

Through Gordon, William Conrad's influence made itself felt among a section of the community that seemed to be chiefly composed of peppery, middle-aged, fox-hunting squires—men who instinctively hated all brass hats, who liked to see people get down to the job and finish it then and there, who played bridge once a week till the early hours of the morning in clubs to which women were not admitted. Through Mr. Malone, it extended to the solid class-conscious society of hall porters, head waiters, taxi drivers, policemen, and shopkeepers—men who, when off duty, dressed like gentlemen and played darts with the solemn air of Guards officers. Through Miss Barker, it reached the white-collar world of typists, secretaries, junior clerks. Through the same channel, it percolated to Flight-Lieutenant W., from whom it subsequently flowed to Jones and finally back to Sir Wallace in the form of flattering reports that left him at his wit's end.

Conrad's internal-propaganda scheme met with success as soon as it was put into operation. In a very short time the authorities noted a marked improvement in the morale of the nation. Every Nazi stratagem was successfully foiled; every lie, false rumor, and disclaimer was refuted and held up to ridicule before it had time to take effect. A sense of unity was soon apparent in every walk of life. The principles of democracy were universally acclaimed, and their value was brought home to every individual citizen. The result of all this was an intensification of effort; the team spirit that had seemed to be on the wane gradually regained ground and was largely responsible for the magnificent exploits that were shortly accomplished.

Much impressed by these immediate results, Churchill sent for Conrad in secret and tendered his warmest congratulations. Conrad felt overwhelmed with pride.

A few minutes after this interview, he was walking home through the blacked-out streets when the air-raid warning sounded. The wail of the sirens was soon succeeded by the noise of falling bombs and antiaircraft fire. It was a heavy raid, heavier than London had experienced for several months. People in the street started making for public shelters and tube stations. A sudden blaze of light that almost blinded Conrad was closely followed by a thunderclap that seemed to burst his ear-drums. That one had landed quite close. A woman who was rushing to take cover was knocked over by the blast, and the child she was carrying in her arms went rolling into the gutter. William Conrad clenched his teeth.

He helped the woman to her feet and picked up the child. Neither was hurt. He saw them safely into the nearest shelter, then automatically started off in the direction of the glow of the incipient fire. In his present state of nervous tension he suddenly remembered his quarrel with the two reporters, and it made him boil with indignation all over again. "To think there are still people in this country who can talk about coming to terms!"

He quickly regained control of himself, of his real self, of Herr Wilhelm Konrad, and was seized by the most bitter remorse. But the mood of the moment was too strong, and he could not shake it off. He finally reached the scene of the explosion. A six-story flat had been reduced to a shapeless pile of blackened stone, twisted metal, and smoldering timber, which blocked most of the street. The fire brigade had already arrived and were trying to confine the flames. The first-aid services were also on the spot, and demolition squads were hard at work. The all clear sounded. People emerged from their holes and gathered round in silence to survey the damage. According to the hall porter of the building, there were a number of residents who never left their flats during a raid and who therefore must have been buried in the rubble. William Conrad broke away from the crowd of onlookers and asked whether he could help.

It was blind fury that impelled him toward the mass of tangled material, which he promptly attacked with pick and shovel and even with his bare hands, hoping that a night of exhausting manual labor would serve to quell the mad desire for revenge that consumed him. His action prompted the rest of the onlookers to follow his example. Several men came forward and, taking up some tools that were not being used, reinforced the working party; then some women joined them and started carting away the rubble. In a few minutes the bomb site was transformed into a vast human anthill, and the head of the demolition squad had to turn away further volunteers—he could not make use of them all.

The work went forward. Bit by bit the metal and charred timbers were removed from the middle of the site and dumped into the corners in four piles that grew visibly larger every second, while what remained of the building slowly began to take shape underneath the half-cleared débris. By daybreak seven crushed bodies had been recovered and carried off, wrapped in blankets. There seemed no hope of finding anyone alive. The crowd of volunteers had been formed into teams working in relays without a moment's pause.

William Conrad had not stopped to rest. He went on digging, tunneling, and scooping as feverishly as ever without the slightest sign of fatigue. With the crowd outside systematically toiling away, he and two other rescue workers pushed forward into the ruins, hacking their way into the heart of the wreckage. There, in the torn bowels of the building, in which fantastic gaps were revealed by the beams of their electric torches, they heard a sort of whimpering noise below them. It seemed to come from a hole in a ceiling where a mass of beams had fallen in. Conrad crept forward along the remains of this surface, which began to give way underneath him. He managed to slip one arm through the splintered slats, but the network of masonry was so thick that his torchlight could not pierce it. Everyone stopped working for a moment to listen, and in the ensuing silence the cry could be heard quite distinctly. There was someone alive down there, but it was going to be a difficult and dangerous job to reach him. Tunneling underneath all this litter might make the whole structure collapse. Considering this risk, the others suggested building a properly reinforced gallery before pushing farther ahead. But Conrad did not listen to them; he had already attacked the woodwork with an ax, and, oblivious of the masonry falling around him, began to lower himself over the jagged edge of the crater. He had taken charge of the whole operation so spontaneously, in a mood that was so contagious, that the others automatically obeyed him without further question.

He told them to fasten a rope round his waist; and by this means, half suspended in mid-air, half straddling the complex of planks and girders, after half an hour's struggle, with his clothes in shreds and his body grazed and bleeding, he managed to get down to the room below. There the havoc was a little less discouraging. The floor boards had come apart, but most of the crossbeams were still in position. The force of the explosion had been expended in destroying the upper stories. In the midst of this chaos the rays of his flashlight came to rest on a bed. It was a child's cot. In flattening out, the metal structure had softened the blow of the huge wooden beam that had fallen across it. The child lying there was trapped underneath, but his eyes were open, and they closed only when dazzled by the rays of the flashlight shining on them.

William Conrad bent down and, with an effort that left him giddy, managed to raise the beam off the child's legs and push the cot clear. He waited a moment or two in an agony of silent dread, and as he stopped to recover his breath under the hail of bricks and plaster pouring down on top of him, he wondered whether in shifting the beam he had not perhaps caused a fatal catastrophe by throwing everything out of balance. He felt the entire structure rock; then the tremor died down, and the whole mass came to rest in a fresh position. By the fading gleam of his flashlight he noticed some dark patches spreading across the bedclothes. The child had opened his eyes again and was looking at him in silence.

He wrapped him in the bloodstained sheets and managed to get him up to the floor above. A quarter of an hour later the victim was being given medical attention. The blood came from a number of superficial cuts caused by splinters from the beam; otherwise he was completely unharmed.

The two men who had been with Conrad described what had happened. The story soon spread through the crowd. Crowds are moved as easily by this sort of exploit as by martial music and public speeches. The shiver of excitement that went through the onlookers foreshadowed a popular display of emotion. They were only waiting for the hero's appearance to break into applause. But William Conrad had vanished.

The head of the rescue squad tried to find him; he wanted his name and address so as to obtain some official recognition of his services. But William Conrad had not given a thought to the reward that might accrue from his impulsive gesture or to the finishing touches it would give to the character he had assumed. With disinterested dignity he had preferred to remain anonymous. So no one who read about the adventure in the newspapers had any idea that he was the central figure in it.

No one, that is, except Sir Wallace and his immediate colleagues, who made it their business to know things that were unknown to the general public.

The news put Sir Wallace into the bad mood that now came over him each time he set his forthright mind to work on this far from forthright case. He was busy studying a thick file forwarded from the political section, in which Conrad's latest work had been gone through with a fine-tooth comb and analyzed in detail. The conclusions reached were more than flattering. The actual results obtained confirmed the objective analysis and justified the popular opinion that the man responsible for this reorganization had certainly deserved well of his country.

As Sir Wallace came to this part of the report, he could not conceal his annoyance. This was the moment Mr. Jones chose to come into his office and inform him that G.Y.22 had distinguished himself yet again by his gallant conduct without even trying to reap any reward for it in the form of publicity. This information had just been given by an agent recently detailed to shadow the eminent author.

Sir Wallace received the news in silence, then put his usual question. "And what do you make of it, Jones?"

Mr. Jones could not say. He had expected this question and had tried in vain to think of an adequate answer. "Well, sir, it seems to be a most extraordinary business—absolutely incomprehensible, sir. Such fiendish deceit—"

Sir Wallace raised his voice by a fraction of a degree. "But you don't really think he's going to carry on like this forever, do you? That he's going to win the war for us all by himself if only he's given the chance? That he's going to cover himself with glory just for the sake of leading us up the garden path—and not even for that, since he's now acting purely gratuitously, as those damned philosophers would say? Do you think that's likely, Jones? Do you think it's the usual habit of Nazi secret agents to risk their lives in order to save every little blue-eyed, curly-haired brat in England? Do you really think so, Jones?"

Mr. Jones was still at a loss and could not reply. Sir Wallace dropped his sarcastic tone and lowered his voice again. "Don't you really admire this fellow's work, Jones? Aren't you absolutely dazzled by his brilliant propaganda scheme? You're not? Then you must be a real exception. Even I have to admit that it's infinitely superior to our ministers' childish efforts. And look at the results it has had. The morale of the country's already much higher. No one can deny that, Jones; I can't and neither can you. So what does it all add up to?

"I'll tell you, Jones. It's simply this: We're groping about in the dark; we haven't the foggiest idea where we are. But if you think I'm going to give up hope and abandon the quest, then all I can say is, Jones, you don't yet know me very well. Sooner or later, I tell you, even the cleverest of them slips up; he will, just like everyone else. There must be something behind all this play acting, this fiendish deceit, as you call it. There must be some definite purpose in the fellow's behavior, and this purpose is obviously of prime importance. You've said so yourself, Jones."

"Yes, sir," Mr. Jones agreed.

"Well, one day we'll know the reason for all this cunning. Perhaps it's because he suspects we've got our eye on him. Perhaps this last gesture of his is only a clever move on the part of a cautious person who knows he's probably being followed and realizes that we're bound to learn about his exploit in spite of his making a point of shunning all publicity."

"Yes, sir, it could be that."

"But you don't seem very convinced, Jones. Well, neither am I. Oh, I know what you're thinking all right. That one can sometimes be a little *too* clever in reading between the lines—isn't that it? But I've told you over and over again, you can't judge these foreigners as you would anyone else. We can't afford to leave a single stone unturned, Jones, and in this country—"

Sir Wallace did not usually talk so much, but there was something about this case that made him break all his normal habits.

"—in this country, Jones, as you know as well as I do, people make mistakes just as often as anywhere else in the world. Our politicians aren't much better than any others, in spite of what we're told; and as for our military leaders, they're such simpletons they make one feel more sorry than angry. But there are at least three factors that explain why we always come out on top, Jones, even in wartime. In the first place, there's our dogged perseverance. It's our best-known quality. I don't mean that our ministers persevere in one particular mistake; what I mean is, they never give up, they persist in following a certain policy and in committing fresh blunders until one of these miraculously leads to a happy result. Our generals never hesitate to go on being defeated, until one day, with the enemy sick and tired of beating us, one of them who is probably a little less dense than the rest suddenly succeeds in turning defeat into victory. That was how we dealt with Napoleon, and our stubbornness will no doubt pull us through again this time. The second factor to which we owe our superiority, Jones, is the efficiency of the service to which you and I have the honor to belong. People don't like us for it, and no wonder. It's not mere chance that our job is known in several languages by the significant name 'intelligence.' We're the brains of the country, Jones, and don't you forget it. If the other sections of the community never bother to think, it's because they rely on us to do their thinking for them. In peacetime this division of labor enables our politicians and business magnates to have a cup of tea at five o'clock every afternoon before going off to play golf or cricket. In wartime it gives our military leaders an excuse for not seeing any farther than the end of their own noses. They know that one day we'll provide enough intelligence to enable even them to beat the enemy. That's one of the reasons we've got to be so strict with ourselves, Jones. One slip on our part could lead to even more serious consequences than the loss of Singapore. A suggestion from this department sometimes has a far greater effect than an order from Whitehall. Look at what Lawrence of Arabia did in the 1914 war." Damn it all, Sir Wallace thought to himself, here I am rambling on exactly like a philosopher; that's what comes of reading all that bloody little don's rubbish!

"Yes, sir," said Mr. Jones.

Sir Wallace went on, carried away by his own eloquence. "Nor is it mere chance, Jones, that the members of our staff are chosen from among the best brains in the country. We demand a standard of natural ability and formal education that you'll hardly ever find in our counterparts elsewhere in the world. On the Continent men of our profession are often recruited from the lowest elements of society, from the underworld and the dregs of the police. That's a bad mistake, a misunderstanding of the character of the service, which is essentially intellectual. With us it's a completely different kettle of fish, as you know as well as I do, since we're both in the same racket.

"As for the third factor that works in our favor, Jones, I don't know whether you're aware of it or not. It took me a long time to realize it myself. It's simply that all this is nothing but a cover; there's something behind it all. But to come back to our particular case. We can't sit back and let an enemy agent give us lessons in our own business. This isn't an ordinary case, Jones, I can tell you. So let's keep on our toes and be ready to catch him out. Meanwhile, we've got to play our cards carefully. By the way, what about that business in the fellow's flat that our friend Beckett wanted taken care of?"

"It's done, sir. Several days ago."

"I presume you made sure that he couldn't have tumbled to it?"

Mr. Jones smiled and did not condescend to answer.

Sir Wallace looked at him and smiled as well. Apart from a few very exceptional occasions demanding unusual psychological insight, for which the service was not normally equipped, every member of the staff could be relied upon to carry out the trickiest operation without making elementary blunders.

PART THREE

17 "*21 March.* Went to party given in his honor by Sir W. and Lady G., after he was invested with George Cross for distinguished services. Seemed very moved by this award.

"*22 March.* Another party in the office, given by the Managing Editor who congratulated him on behalf of the staff. Replied in the same spirit.

"*25 March.* Wrote to Major A. P. Copy from Censor attached. No comments."

"Why can't that brute Jones vary his remarks a bit?" grumbled Sir Wallace.

"*Contacts:* Nothing fresh to report. Miss B. still absorbed in her work. Lady G. attending casualties two nights a week and devoting rest of time to welfare work; has dismissed her maid, who, at her suggestion, has since joined up; does all the housework herself. Sir W. no longer buying whisky from usual source."

"If this chap's allowed to remain at large for another year," muttered Sir Wallace, inflamed with spite, "every babe in arms will be transformed into a fully armed warrior, their mothers will be making tanks and flame throwers, our Conservative M.P.'s will all be drinking water, and the Old Man himself will have given up his cigars! To hell with all this nonsense! Let's see what he has to say in his letter."

"My dear Arthur,

"Congratulations on your promotion. Although you don't say much about it, I imagine your little cruise in the Chinese junk must have been rather out of the ordinary. I must say, I envy you. I'd give anything to be on active service again. Meanwhile, old boy, I'm rapidly developing into a bloody bureaucrat, which makes me a little ashamed when I realize what other people are doing. It's interesting work, of course. I was fascinated by it at first; and I think it's really doing some good. But there are moments when I feel I'd like to chuck the whole thing and see some action again, no matter where. I honestly mean it. As it is, I often feel I can stand it no longer.

"I hope you're in Australia by now and that this letter will reach you soon. I quite agree with you about the general situation. The ground we've lost isn't as important as all that, and we'll easily recover it as soon as—"

Sir Wallace was interrupted in his reading by the sudden appearance of Mr. Jones. Mr. Jones had just arrived from outside and was out of breath. Although he knew his chief was in the office, he had not knocked on the door before coming in. Sir Wallace realized at once that something important must have happened.

"I've got some news for you, sir," gasped Mr. Jones.

The visit to Conrad's flat had been accomplished with the greatest of ease. The writer had no idea that one evening when he was busy in the office two young men had broken into his rooms and made a note of his reference books.

To make sure that they were not surprised in the act, Mr. Malone and his wife had been taken off to Scotland Yard by genuine policemen unconsciously collaborating with these bogus burglars. Following the instructions he had received from a very high authority, an inspector interrogated them both for a long time on the subject of an alleged relative of theirs who had been up to no good. Mrs. Malone was scared out of her wits. Mr. Malone, with a perfectly clear conscience, started off by protesting his innocence and disclaiming all knowledge of the matter; but the inspector's attitude and cleverly framed questions gradually inveigled him into making several contradictory statements, and he soon lost much of his self-assurance. This went on for two hours. Both the Malones were beginning to be almost convinced themselves that they had somehow committed a serious offense when the inspector received a short telephone call, at the end of which he apologized profusely, saying there had been some unfortunate confusion in names, that in wartime it was sometimes necessary to use rather drastic methods, but that the Malones were now free to leave at once. He made them promise, however, in the interests of the country, not to breathe a word about the interrogation. Mr. Malone nobly accepted his apology and with the air of a man upholding the Official Secrets Act swore not to mention it to a soul.

The two young men who took such an interest in Conrad's books were sufficiently badly dressed and carried such compromising tools in their pockets as to be able to pass themselves off as ordinary burglars in case anything went wrong with their plans. They were past masters at this sort of search. To them it was child's play. The small size of the rooms and the scarcity of furniture made the job all the easier. They needed no more than half an hour to make certain that there were only three reference books in the flat: an English-Polish lexicon, a French-Polish lexicon, and a 1924 edition of the *Pocket Oxford Dictionary.*

The younger of the two callers then produced a notebook and took dictation from his companion, who was evidently in charge of the operation:

"1. *English-Polish Lexicon, 1919.* Well-used, several pages dog-eared, ink-stained. Childish doodling on endpapers. Hasty examination revealed no further distinguishing features.

"2. *Polish-French Lexicon, 1920.* Same condition. Same comments.

"3. *Pocket Oxford Dictionary, 1924.* Brand-new. Unmarked. Seems to open more easily at first half."

Having completed his mission, the leader of the expedition put the books back in their place, made sure that nothing else had been moved, and gave the signal to leave. An hour later, J. R. Beckett was in possession of the information. It was a fortnight after this that Mr. Jones burst into Sir Wallace's office in a most unusual state of excitement and breathlessly reported that he had some news.

"What sort of news, Jones?" Sir Wallace inquired, trying hard to conceal his own excitement.

"Several things, sir, all rather important. But this is

the main point, I think. I've just been to see Beckett. I thought you'd like to know at once that you were quite right: The letter did contain a hidden message. Beckett has done the trick, sir. He has broken the code. He says the solution's quite positive. Here's the message, sir: 'Good work. Carry on. Your long patience soon rewarded.' "

Mr. Jones recovered his composure a little.

"I apologize for this rough note, sir. Beckett just scribbled it down. I told him it wasn't worth typing out, sir, as I wanted you to see it at once."

"The bloody swine!" exclaimed Sir Wallace. "Didn't I tell you we'd catch him out in the end? Beckett's absolutely certain, I hope?"

"Quite positive, sir. Those were his very words."

"The bloody swine, Jones! The dirty double-crosser! Even I was beginning to have my doubts and feel almost ashamed of suspecting him. What will the Government say when they hear their splendid reorganization was planned and more or less put into operation by a German spy? But they'll probably never know. You were saying, Jones, you've got other important news for me?"

"Yes, sir. Before going to Beckett's, I called in at the Censor's. They gave me a copy of two letters that have just arrived for Conrad. One's from a battalion commander in the Far East reporting the death of Conrad's friend Arthur Patton. That's a mere incidental, sir; there's nothing in it. But the other one, sir, the second letter, comes from the same source as the original message. No doubt about it; same handwriting, same style. These letters haven't yet been delivered. I took steps to prevent the second one being sent, even though I had no authority. But I thought you would first like to know what was in it, sir. Beckett's bound to be able to decipher it if it's in the same code. I gave him the letter, sir, and he's working on it now. If there's nothing for me to do here at the moment, I'll go back and see if there's any result to report, sir."

"Good God, Jones, jump to it! Here we are gossiping away and meanwhile he might have discovered—Quick, Jones, get a move on!"

Mr. Jones was outside in a flash. Sir Wallace tried to curb his impatience by glancing through the letter from the Far East. In his anxiety to know how everything was going to turn out, he found it almost impossible to concentrate:

". . . so I'm writing to you, as I know you were one of his best friends. . . . One of the finest officers in the unit . . . deeply missed by all his comrades-in-arms . . . hemmed in on all sides by the Japanese . . . when all the ammunition was exhausted . . . killed by a sabre-stroke after fierce hand-to-hand fighting. . . ."

Preoccupied though he was, Sir Wallace could not help thinking of Patton and tried to imagine the scene: the Japs creeping up through the undergrowth; the ineffective bursts of submachine-gun fire; the last hand grenades; then nothing but a pistol; and finally, right at the end, a knife—that was part of the normal equipment out there. He felt a lump in his throat. He had so often cursed the little don for his letters that he had come to regard him almost with affection.

"I bet some brilliant idea was burgeoning in his brain

the very moment he was hacked to pieces! Poor little blighter! No more Archaeopteryx as far as he's concerned!"

"An idealist; an ideologist; a simple chap at heart, no doubt, like all those intellectuals; quite unaware of this business, just a friend who had been taken in by the devilish cunning of a traitor. Jones is right—a mere incidental; nothing in it at all. But I wish that fellow Jones would hurry up and come back," Sir Wallace concluded.

Nothing remained but to add this letter to the others in the file. It brought to a definite close the series of idle digressions that had clouded the main issue. It was best not to think about them any longer now that this main issue seemed on the point of being brought to light.

Mr. Jones had returned flourishing the new message:

"*29 March. 20.30 hrs.* Dine alone Ritz restaurant. Stranger will contact."

"There we are, sir. It looks as if they've decided to make a move at last."

"What did I tell you, Jones? Sooner or later even the cleverest of them slips up somewhere. G.Y.22's bound to slip up now, unless, of course, he takes no action at all. You see? But let's keep our wits about us. The end isn't yet in sight, not by a long chalk. We've still got to find out what's behind all this; and so far we haven't an idea. We've got to let them nibble at the bait, him and the unknown correspondent and maybe others as well, and pull them all in when they're well and truly hooked."

"The twenty-ninth, that's two days from now, sir. I suppose I can give the necessary instructions to have the letter delivered to him tomorrow morning?"

"Certainly, Jones. And whom do you think we ought to send to the Ritz to keep tabs on the mysterious stranger?"

Mr. Jones quickly outlined a plan of campaign.

"Well, sir, we've got one of the waiters there working for us; he could report anything he overheard. It wouldn't be much, I'm afraid. He's quite a bright lad and absolutely secure; a useful chap to have in a big hotel, sir. But that's not quite good enough. Duncan's not exactly the type for this sort of work. . . . Let's see now, whom else have we got? Yes, I think he's the very man—Heyst, sir. He's pretty shrewd; he's also inconspicuous; he could shadow anyone without being noticed."

"All right, Jones. I'll leave you to settle the details. Don't forget the security factor. It's still just as important as ever."

Sir Wallace had nothing further to add and got up to leave. He glanced at the safe and at the same time, by association of ideas, felt for the bunch of keys in his pocket; then he put on his hat. Mr. Jones was about to say good night when Sir Wallace suddenly remembered something, something important he had almost overlooked.

"Would you please ring up Beckett for me, Jones."

Mr. Jones dialed a number and handed Sir Wallace the receiver.

"Hello, Beckett? Do you recognize my voice? Were you asleep already?"

"Yes, sir—I mean, not yet, sir!"

"I just wanted to say good night, Beckett, and to let you know I'm pretty pleased with the way you've managed things. Not a bad show at all. It's only what I expected of you, though. Well, good night, Beckett."

Sir Wallace hung up.

"That goes for you too, Jones. Jolly good show. Keep it up and we'll see this business through to the end. It's in the interests of the country, don't forget. Good night to you, Jones."

"Good night, sir," said Mr. Jones with a slight bow.

18

Miss Barker, who had left the office at three o'clock that morning, was back at work again at eight. She wanted to finish typing the final draft of the Foreign Agents' Instructions before the author of that document came in. This was the last of the work. The reorganization was now complete. There was nothing more to be done but wait for developments. Conrad had told her to take a few days off after this final effort. At first she had refused, but he persuaded her by saying that he did not want to see her again until the circles under her eyes had disappeared. She was happy to be finishing the work and planned to make the most of her leave, which she felt she had really earned.

"You're early, Joan," said Conrad as he came in. "Not too tired, I hope? What have you got for me this morning?"

"Nothing much, sir. It's nearly finished. There are two personal letters for you."

He looked at the envelopes, and his heart gave a leap

as he recognized the handwriting on the first one. Then he noticed the B.A.P.O. stamp on the second—Patton, obviously—and was amazed at being confronted once again with the two separate halves of his double life, brought together in the morning's mail.

He opened the C.O.'s letter and read the first sentence, which announced the death of Arthur Patton. At first he could not grasp the meaning of the words that were plainly written there. It was only by degrees, slowly and painfully, that he came to realize the true significance of this irreparable stroke of fate. His friend's death was the climax to a succession of emotions that had first undermined and finally shattered his resistance. Once again he felt he was a mere puppet, being crushed under the weight of an impression.

This impression, which had been growing on him for months, which had been nourished by countless unimportant little incidents of his everyday life, which he had had so much difficulty in shaking off on New Year's Eve, he now felt to be lodged in his brain for good.

The strange world into which his vocation had cast him a few years before had been slowly encroaching on his personality, its insidious influence mounting round him like the waters of a flood. And now that he was finally going under, even though he realized he was vanquished and had lost his individuality forever, he still could not understand how he had come to give in to this terrible compulsion—he of all people, whose former self would have dismissed such petty incidents with a scornful smile.

But he had had no means of defending himself against them. There was no effective antidote for him to fall back on as a result of his education and upbringing, and he did not have the instinct to rebel. He was just a barbarian. His lords and masters were barbarians. His god was a barbarian, who boasted of launching armed hordes against a crumbling civilization in order to build a new world out of bloodshed and corruption.

Like all barbarians, Conrad took everything too seriously. His mind could not view anything with detachment but was guided by the brute force of logic and fanaticism. He could never close his eyes and disregard the influence of those to whom he was united by the bonds of friendship. He never smiled. The most commonplace sentiments, the experience of a little affection, the sight of a little good will, the most time-worn clichés, all these found a fruitful breeding ground in his elementary brain. A civilized man would have been better armed, but he had been brought up on raw meat. He had never savored the sweet milk of frivolity, the aromatic honey of irony, the salt of good-humored wit, which centuries of so-called corruption had bred in the hearts of more sophisticated people. He was blind to the latest triumphs of wisdom or decadence. In his eyes any form of human kindness had an ulterior motive behind it.

In forging Conrad's armor, the disciples of Nietzsche had overlooked the penetrating power of human kindness. They had taught him only what they knew themselves. They were expert in the use of violence and subterfuge. They had instructed him in every known form of torture without omitting the smallest detail, not only in order to familiarize him with the infinite variety of their particular field of activity but also to put him on his guard against the excruciating effect of sudden pain.

Several times in the course of his intensive training, theoretical instruction had been followed by practical demonstration. Being acquainted, then, with the most hideous aspects of torture, and knowing the limits of his own endurance, he was not afraid of it. He knew that a strong-willed person could stand any amount of ill treatment without flinching; and against the more refined forms of torture the pill he always carried secreted on his person was a certain safeguard. He was also proof against mental persuasion. His instructors had given him so many instances of it that he would never have yielded to it. What they had overlooked, however, was the sweet, insidious influence of ordinary everyday impressions. Perhaps they denied the possibility of such an influence. Perhaps they had no idea it even existed, since they themselves had never been exposed to its undermining effects. Perhaps ordinary everyday impressions were unknown in their country, alien to their way of life, incompatible with the oppressive atmosphere of pomp and sacrifice, which the knights of the *Nibelungenlied* and the demigods of Valhalla had to breathe if they were to fulfill their glorious destiny.

The symbol of Siegfried was lost on them. They had not taught Conrad that every suit of armor had a sensitive area, which might possibly be proof against fear and pain but which nevertheless let in impressions. Once these impressions had taken root, they formed malignant humors which spread like gangrene. Was this sensitive area situated over the heart or in the brain? Was its comparative weakness due to the irresistible pressure of an overpowering environment? Was the main feature of this environment its undermining quality, as Patton used to claim? Or else had these humors been lying dormant and unsuspected within Conrad ever since his conception, as a result of the peculiar quality of the molecules that had gone into the making of his chromosomes? Was there, in fact, a weak point in his armor, an area more vulnerable than the rest? Or was it the whole suit that was of inferior quality, built of a shoddy material which, like a bad painting under the effect of heat, buckled, came apart, and slowly fell to pieces when submitted to a few feeble impressions of human decency?

Had he by his own attitude helped to spread these insidious poisons? Had he distilled them, he alone, by pretending to put his natural ability and good will at the disposal of the free world? Pretending to, indeed! Was there now any question of pretense? A daily struggle! A real battle! His own personal battle! That was how his activity during the years he had lived in this country now appeared to him. His chiefs had said, "You are to fuse your own life into the life of those decadents. You will copy their gestures and imitate their manner of speech. You will force yourself to behave and to talk as they do. You will induce them to recognize in you a reflection of themselves."

Conrad had obeyed. He had obeyed with his usual devotion to duty. Was it his fault that this devotion had eventually grown into a natural inclination? From the very start he had forced himself to rebel against his personal impressions, to despise these enemies who assailed him all the more violently by assuming forms it was impossible to hate: Patton, Lady Goodfellow, Miss Barker, Gordon, Mr. Malone, and even those elderly gentlemen whose very ingenuousness and elementary snobbery afforded him no room for contempt. He had bolstered up this natural inclination of his by his public utterances. He had been obliged to do so; it was part of his duty. Had he not thereby succeeded in convincing even the most distrustful of his audience? But he had not been able to resist the force of his own argument. His conscience had been overwhelmed by his eloquence and logical dexterity.

Without thinking, Conrad put the letter from Patton's C.O. in his pocket, together with the other one, which he could not even be bothered to open, then started going through Miss Barker's typescript. He worked in his usual methodical fashion, making a few corrections, crossing out an occasional word and substituting another. His secretary noticed nothing abnormal in his behavior. His emotion lay deep down inside him; there was no change in his outward appearance; he was used to concealing his feelings.

". . . a hero's death . . . hand-to-hand fighting in the jungle. . . ."

The memory of his friend came sharply into focus against the background of relentless impressions. These shreds of humanity, as tenuous as ghosts, had been sufficiently powerful to transform an academic idealist into a fighting soldier. Scorn them, indeed! Was there perhaps some hidden quality, some concealed strength in this nation which was outwardly so commonplace; some basic essential, which was manifest only in the guise of Lady Goodfellow's smile, Miss Barker's neat efficiency, Mr. Malone's dignified bearing, the boyish high spirits of these adult cricket players?

He handed the sheets back to Miss Barker.

"That's all right, Joan. Just a few alterations. Would you please make the corrections straightaway? Then I'll be able to get it off at once."

". . . One of the finest officers in the unit . . . deeply missed by all his comrades-in-arms. . . ."

Few men could have hated the prospect of soldiering more than Patton. Yet the mere threat to the world he admired and the liberty he loved had been sufficient for him to learn and finally excel in the science of arms. He had joined up at a time when not a soul in this stronghold of freedom would have dreamed of forcing him to enlist. Churchill had eventually expanded conscription to take in almost every able-bodied man, but only because the people had more or less demanded it. The full consent, the approval of the nation had been required before the boldest and most popular man in England dared take this step.

"Sir," said Miss Barker coming up with one of the sheets in her hand, "I can't quite make out this bit. I'm sorry, but there's so much crossed out. . . ."

"Let's have a look, Joan. 'The ridiculous lies of Nazi propaganda. . . .' All clear now?"

"All clear, sir, thank you."

Had he been defeated by purely imaginary enemies? A few formal gestures? A few arbitrary attitudes? Some pointless traditions? A way of life that might just as easily have assumed some other form? Or was there, as Patton had suggested, some communal spiritual store, built up in the course of the centuries; a sacred core, which could afford to be frivolous by virtue of its age and tenacity; a substance that resulted from the normal passage of mankind through time and space; an intellectual principle of which these gestures were nothing more than the mysterious symbols, of which these attitudes were only the reflection?

Where did the strength of this principle lie? By what

secret mechanism did an abstract idea give birth to such power? How was it that these narrow-minded gentlemen always succeeded in imposing their petty opinions on the highest and mightiest on earth? Why, after being defeated on the field of battle, overwhelmed by superior science and strategy, and routed on every front, did they always manage to have the last word? Hamstrung by outworn tradition, slow to adapt themselves, unimaginative in conception and clumsy in execution, determined to suffer every consequence of their mistakes before finally abandoning them, improvident in time of peace, shirking work as far as possible, overflowing with energy for their childish games, hypocritical and selfish in their pleasures, sentimental after their own fashion, idealists, ideologists, simple-minded, punctilious, and slow-witted, by what magic did they always reduce every conqueror on earth to despair? What fair-whiskered, fireless archangel led this flock through defeat after defeat to ultimate victory? What God in these overcast northern skies attended them in their scandalous triumph?

Conrad no longer tried to find the answer. His only anxiety now was to wind up the whole business. One could not live with impunity for months on end in the middle of a paradox; he was tired to death and only longed to escape. The rationalist in him demanded a logical conclusion to this hopelessly confused situation. He realized with a bitter smile that this conclusion would come about of its own accord, as a result of the sequence of events that had led him in his weakness to surrender. If he did not have some last-minute change of heart, his ultimate fate was inevitable. He would probably end up by marrying Miss Barker or some other blue-eyed English miss, building a home where the cult of individual liberty would be practiced, and raising a family of cricketers on the principle of the greatest happiness of the greatest number!

But the enthusiast saw another way out for him—a solution that was compatible with his pride; an outcome that was worthy of his tragic state; a last gesture, which, while fitting in perfectly with the extravagant ideas of the society in which he was now immured, would still be in accordance with the notions of honor he had inherited from his ancestors. He foresaw this gesture as clearly as though it were already a thing of the past. It was prompted by the need to damn himself still further, by the urge to add the final touch of madness to the clashing colors that had been piled onto the canvas of his fate, to turn this canvas into a grotesque daub so that neither god nor man would be able to make out the original design.

He had finished his work. He got up to leave.

"Well, that's over, Joan. I don't want to see you again for at least another week. I've spoken to Mr. Gordon, and he agrees. In any case I'm going to take a few days off myself. And I'm afraid I shan't be able to lunch with you today; I've an urgent appointment. We've worked well together, haven't we? Good-by, Joan, have a good time."

Conrad went back to his flat. Before going out, he had applied for an interview with someone in the War Office who he knew would help him, for another interview with an official in the Ministry of Propaganda. He thought the matter over again. He had come to a definite decision, but there were various possible means of carrying out the project he had in mind. It was Mr. Malone who finally decided him.

Mr. Malone greeted him on the doorstep with, "Seen the papers, sir? There seems to be quite a lot going on in the Western Desert. Heavy reinforcements arriving for us almost every week. I shouldn't be surprised if the general offensive was launched out there any day now. Good news, isn't it, sir?"

"Extremely good, Mr. Malone."

"With the jolly old Russians holding their own in Europe, if we push forward on the other front, it might be the turning of the tide, sir."

"I certainly hope so . . . the turning of the tide, as you say, Mr. Malone."

Conrad went up to his flat. He had come home with the urgent desire to be alone and read about his friend's death in private. He took the C.O.'s letter out of his pocket, and with it the other letter that had come at the same time.

He had completely forgotten it. It now brought back to him all the petty incidentals that had distracted his mind and slowed down his pace by forcing him to deal with more than one thing at a time. He could not bear the sight of this rectangle of paper, which was trying to come between him and the decision he had taken. He did not even open it. He tore it up, envelope and all, and threw the pieces into the wastepaper basket without even bothering to burn them.

19 The next evening, before half past eight, Sir Wallace was sitting by himself at a table in the less conspicuous corner of the Ritz restaurant. He, of course, was not to take any active part in the business, but he had decided to be on the spot. He was too impatient, he had taken too much trouble over this scoundrel, he could not resist the temptation to see him and his unknown partner fall into his net. The headwaiter had not been surprised to hear a respectable, solitary, middle-aged gentleman ask for the recess usually reserved for wary unmarried couples, or on occasion, at least, couples unmarried to one another. In these days of restrictions, respectable, solitary, middle-aged gentlemen could seek little extra luxuries in big restaurants and did not wish to be noticed at that pursuit. From here, behind cleverly arrayed green plants, Sir Wallace could observe the whole huge dining room with very little risk of being seen by his prey. Besides, if by any hard luck this did occur, here also the excuse of Lady Goodfellow's husband was too evident. He had only to wink and say, man to man, not to utter a word to his wife of this solitary debauch.

The other actors, except the mysterious correspondent, were known to him through their photographs although they did not know him. He was delighted with this and prepared himself to view the spectacle with the intransigeant eye of the impresario. He had noticed Heyst sitting in the lobby outside the restaurant apparently engrossed in a newspaper. He had approved of the suitable clothes he was wearing and of his perfectly natural attitude. The agent was evidently waiting for Conrad to come in and be shown to his table. Sir Wallace silently applauded the subtle manner in which he appeared to be utterly absorbed in the evening's news. Everything was under control in that direction; Jones had chosen the most suitable man for the job.

He also recognized the waiter who came to take his order. The latter, of course, had no idea that he was serving someone who was a redoubtable figure for many people, including those in high places; nor did he suspect that the report he was to send to a mysterious address later that evening would be read, before being filed away, by this rather imposing customer who was taking so much interest in the menu.

Sir Wallace ordered the best meal that could be had within the five-shilling limit the austerity regulations enforced on every restaurant in the country. Because of their cosmopolitan clientele, however, establishments like the Ritz were still allowed to provide extras over and above that price, including drinks, coffee, and liqueurs in unlimited quantities. He ordered a pint of beer and began drinking it as he glanced round the room. Here, as in most public places, an attempt had been made to keep up appearances. The hors d'oeuvres were *varié* only in name, but they were served by waiters in tailcoats; and the cutlery surrounding each plate would have sufficed for a banquet.

The room gradually filled up. There were a number of foreigners, mostly Americans—staff officers, war correspondents, and businessmen—the advance guard of the transatlantic armada that had at last decided to come over and tidy up the situation in Europe. There were also a few British officers on leave, who could hardly be blamed for choosing a luxury hotel in which to spend their fortnight off duty. The mystery man was possibly one of these. Sir Wallace began to scrutinize each one in turn but soon gave up such a fruitless pastime.

Nine o'clock already; Conrad was late. Sir Wallace was beginning to get impatient. But it was only his imagination; he had been looking forward to this meeting so much that he had arrived much too early, so as to make sure of being there before the unknown contact turned up. He started to eat, but his initial euphoria had vanished.

Half past nine; in the circumstances such a delay was inconceivable. Here was yet another of those worrying, inexplicable factors that had clouded the whole damned case from the very start.

Ten o'clock. Sir Wallace forced himself to take as long as possible to eat a sweet that was not sweet. Heyst had just come in and chosen a table. Once again Sir Wallace silently applauded him. There was nothing in his behavior to rouse the slightest suspicion. Heyst had sat down in a spot where he could see everyone in the room; with his paper at his elbow, he still looked as pensive and withdrawn as ever. It was not his fault. It was nobody's fault. It was a perfectly planned operation, but some unexpected factor must have thrown the whole thing out of gear—some capricious fancy on the part of an evil spirit, which Sir Wallace was furious to find beyond his comprehension.

He left the restaurant at eleven o'clock. The room was almost empty. The only customers left were Heyst, who was quietly finishing his meal, and a party of Americans chatting in loud tones, which intensified his irritation. But he managed to conceal the bad mood he was in under a heavy display of good humor and well-being. Neither the waiter who wished him good night nor the cloakroom attendant who helped him into his overcoat could have guessed what he was really feeling. He even went so far as to overtip them both, in the manner of a gentleman who had dined well and so felt inclined to be expansive. This was a private affair and did not concern the outside world. Sir Wallace looked forward to seeing Mr. Jones in private to tell him what he thought of the evening's entertainment.

But Mr. Jones gave him neither the time nor the opportunity to vent his feelings. Without even waiting to be summoned he burst into the Director's office, showing an unfortunate lack of manners, which the monstrous absurdity of this case tended to bring more and more into evidence. Bowled over by an unpredictable stroke of fate, Mr. Jones was on the verge of tears.

"Have you heard the latest, sir? Yes, I know; he never kept the appointment—Heyst has just rung me up. But that's not all, sir, not by a long chalk. He has joined up again, sir! This information has only just come in. He has enlisted for the duration! With the rank of captain, sir! He has handed in his resignation to the Propaganda Department in spite of all the Minister's efforts to keep him on. He said that his mind was made up and that no one in this country could oppose an individual's sense of duty! That the main part of his propaganda work was done and any old fool could deal with the rest! He said the war was now approaching its climax—'the turning of the tide,' those were his very words, sir. He said that the moment had come for drastic action, and that a young and experienced officer like himself ought to be ashamed of himself if he did not take part in it. That's what he said, sir! He pulled every string to get himself posted to the Western Desert in a tank regiment. As a common-or-garden captain, sir! He leaves for the Middle East in a few days."

20

In taking this final decision, Conrad had completely recovered his former will power. Nothing had been able to deter him, neither Lady Goodfellow's tears, nor Miss Barker's pleading glances, nor Gordon's fury, nor Sir Wallace's fatherly advice, nor the opinion of the highest authorities. He had barely consented to stay on a fortnight longer so as to hand over the job to his successor. Then he had gone off, leaving his friends behind and taking with him only his memories.

Those memories remained with him in the desert. Though armed conflict could not rid him of his impressions, it did at least relieve their bitterness. Fighting restored his peace of mind. The step he had taken had enabled him to get over his mental qualms and twinges of conscience. He saw his recent past in the form of a sequence of images that he could recall without a pang of remorse. The final ritual had been a party given in his honor just before he left, at which all his friends had gathered round him and sung "For He's a Jolly

Good Fellow," while he had felt once more deeply moved.

During the endless succession of advances and withdrawals that were the main feature of the Western Desert campaign, he gave further proof of his gallantry, and further mentions added to his glory. On October 20, 1942, Lieutenant-Colonel William Conrad was in command of a mechanized unit in front of El Alamein, preparing for the assault that was to lead to the barbarians' downfall. Suddenly an attack was launched by German tanks that broke through the Allied lines and, pushing forward in a number of spearheads, caused a certain amount of local confusion, which threatened to disrupt the preparations of several months. At this unexpected blow, Middle East Command almost gave up its original plan and seriously considered fighting a rearguard action to fresh positions farther back. William Conrad saved the situation. As he had done at Dunkirk, but with even greater firmness, thanks to his senior rank, he stuck to his guns, rallied the units in retreat, and reorganized them in a strong defensive position; then, without waiting for orders, which in any case never arrived, he launched his armored cars against the oncoming enemy and succeeded in cutting them off from their base. This was the decisive move that turned a critical situation into a brilliant victory. Its consequences were incalculable. The German tanks were wiped out, the counter-attack was brought to a standstill, and the enemy morale badly shaken. Rommel's star was on the wane. The British lines were re-established and reinforced with strong points. The full-scale Allied advance started from this position three days later.

But Colonel William Conrad was no longer there to receive the laurels he had won through this latest exploit. A bullet fired out of the barbarian world, his own world, pierced his suit of armor and put an end to the paradox of his glory. This was the logical outcome he had chosen. In the last transport of delirium before his final rest he remained conscious long enough to remember his childhood vow and to rejoice at having made the supreme sacrifice by dying like a hero for the cause of his country.

The news of his death was received with silent emotion by the little group of friends who had unconsciously played a leading part in the development of his career. Their emotion was essentially private; no tears were shed. A real gentleman never gave way to his feelings. With Lady Goodfellow it was simply a case of misty eyes, a silent prayer, then down to work again with redoubled energy. With Sir Wallace, a short address followed by a minute's silence round the table. With Gordon, a blasphemy or two. With Mr. Malone, a solemn announcement to his wife that one of the finest men in the land had just lost his life. With Miss Barker, a photograph of Conrad in uniform—one of the few in existence—piously nailed to the wall in her bedroom, a few inches below the picture of Princess Elizabeth and His Majesty King George. God save His Gracious Majesty! God save him for his subjects for as long as He sees fit, gracious so as to give no offense, victorious as a result of tradition, and happy before being glorious!

As usual Sir Wallace had been the first informed. He had never given up. Ever since William Conrad's re-enlistment the G.Y.22 file had been kept up-to-date with countless reports, all of which sung the hero's praises, making much of his selfless conduct and fine behavior. As usual it was Mr. Jones who announced the news.

When he learned of this latest development, Sir Wallace felt the veil being torn from his eyes. At this stage of the mystery, when a spade could at last be called a spade, he lost control of himself for the first time in his life. He burst into a spate of invective. It was as though all the effort he had put into this case had been distilled into a highly inflammable spirit, which was now set off by the striking of a match. His thoughts poured out like boiling lava, in a stream of expressions he would normally never have dreamed of using in front of his subordinates, his voice betraying an odd mixture of temper and affection. Mr. Jones was overwhelmed by an avalanche of sound, a cataract of speech, in which the words "bloody," "blasted," and "bastard," not to mention a number of others still more violent, gave evidence of the incomparable richness of the English language and the utter indignation of his chief.

"The bastard was genuine, Jones! Can you imagine it? He was absolutely genuine! Like a silly, bloody fool I never tumbled to it before, and here we've been wallowing for months in a mystery that didn't exist, devoting more time and trouble to this lunatic than to all the other scoundrels in Europe. He was quite sincere! I'll be damned if I thought it possible. Would you believe it, Jones? Here's a bloody bastard of a German spy, yet he has done more for King and Country than all our chaps put together! He died for our cause—and in all sincerity, Jones, I tell you!

"He was well and truly won over, completely converted, brought to his knees by the damnable atmosphere of virtue that this bloody kingdom and empire of ours seem to exhale. Do you realize what that means, Jones? The silly fool was absolutely crushed by the weight of our wonderful perfection. He couldn't take it, Jones. The experience was too much for him. His heart was melted by the singing of our gallant little Tommies, by the pigheaded stupidity of our idiotic generals, by the virtue, devotion, and knitting needles of our gracious ladies, by the shabby suits of the silly chumps in the House of Lords, by the cheerful efficiency of our pert little typists, by the ravings of our damn fools of philosophers, by the pretty little speeches of our darling little Princess. Who'd have believed such utter bloody nonsense?

"Yes, Jones, he was genuine, all right. He gradually came to realize that if there was any bloody justice in the world, it was to be found on our side. After repeating this over and over again month after month, he ended up by believing it himself and found himself, in his silly, mad, foreign way, completely won over by our virtues! By our virtues, Jones, can you believe it? And once he was convinced of them, he decided quite simply to sacrifice his youth, talent, and life's blood in the cause of liberty! Just like that—simply by following the example of all the other admirable idiots in this wonderful country of ours!

"And do you know what's going to happen now, Jones? He's going to be covered with medals and posthumous awards. Twenty years from now, Jones, in twenty years' time I bet you every silly little snob over here will be worshiping his name as much as the memory of Wellington or even Nelson! And do you know the really extraordinary thing about all this, Jones? I'm not going to do a thing about it. I shan't breathe a word, not to a single soul!

"This is the last I want to hear about this business, Jones. I don't ever want to be reminded of it again. A silly romantic ass, that's what he was, Jones. This service can't waste time over raving lunatics like that. After all, we're a perfectly sane and properly organized body of adult men. And if we start thinking that a bloody swine isn't always a bloody swine or that a dirty little traitor can sometimes behave like a gentleman, even though he's double-crossing both sides at the same time, then our job would be utterly impossible. So remember, Jones. I always told you there was something fishy about this business . . . and look where it has landed us. Let it be a lesson to you, Jones. You can never, repeat never, be certain of anything when you're dealing with a blasted foreigner. . . ."

Having delivered this funeral oration and thereby relieved his feelings, Sir Wallace did his best to recover his normal air of detachment, as befitted a man in his position. Having partly succeeded, he said good night to Mr. Jones and left the office at a somewhat brisker pace than usual.

"Good night, sir," said Mr. Jones.

The young man remained deep in thought for a minute or two, then began putting out the lights before going into his room next door. But in the middle of this final ritual he suddenly gasped with alarm and stood rooted to the floor while a look of abject horror crept over his face.

He made a dive for the door, rushed through the corridor like a whirlwind, dashed down the stairs, and started running like a madman until he caught sight of his chief at the end of the street.

"Sir! Sir!" gasped Mr. Jones.

Sir Wallace turned round. "What's up now?" he demanded.

"The safe, sir! The safe's still open!"

Sir Wallace could have kicked himself. It was quite true; in his agitation he had forgotten to lock the top-secret safe.

James T. Farrell

☐ A BRAND NEW LIFE

The scene is Prohibition Chicago of 1928. The time is just before the big crash. Newly divorced Anne Daniels arrives in Chicago and meets Roger Raymond, and begins a new life. James T. Farrell has written more than thirty books and is considered one of America's foremost writers.

(#15111—$1.50)

☐ INVISIBLE SWORDS

A powerful novel of universal appeal concerning a crumbling marriage jeopardized by the birth of a deformed child. The *Saturday Review* called this one of Farrell's most powerful novels. Mr. Farrell handles a delicate subject with rare insight into the minds of a husband and wife. (#15106—$1.50)

MB Books, P.O. Box 298, Franklin Square, N.Y. 11010
Please send me the MB Books I have checked above. I am enclosing $__________(check or money order, no currency or C.O.D.s). Enclose price listed for each title plus 15¢ per copy ordered to cover cost of postage and handling.

For an order form for all Manor Book titles, write to the above address.

Name ______________________________

Address ______________________________

City ____________ State __________ Zip Code ______

(This offer expires January, 1975)